HOLLOW
REGALIA

01
Corpse
Reviver

GAKUTO
MIKUMO

Illustration by
MIYUU

HOLLOW
REGALIA

Miwa Waon

CHARACTERS

Josh

Yang Wei

Paola

Moujuu Tamer

Iroha Mamana

Galerie Berith:

European trading company. They mostly deal in weapons and military technology. This deadly dealer has its own private military for protection. Funded by the House of Berith.

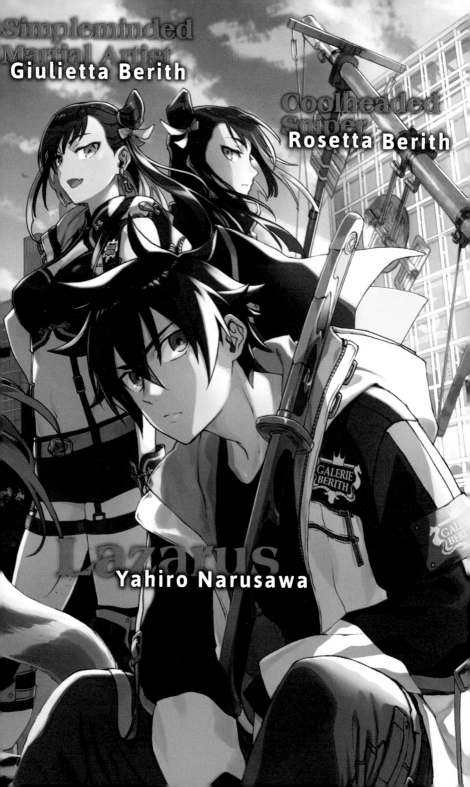

Simpleminded Martial Artist
Giulietta Berith

Coolheaded Sniper
Rosetta Berith

Lazarus
Yahiro Narusawa

"Enjoy your dreams while they last, Deadly Maiden."

The count turned his back on Nathan, hiding his restlessness and disappointment. He glanced to the slumbering test subject beyond the glass before exiting the room, saying:

The white-haired girl continued to smile faintly as she slept.

"Unfortunately, Count, we still have a long way to go before her awakening, and we need a conscious weapon in order to bring about a new disaster."

"So we have no choice but to capture the Kushinada... Fine. I will see you around, Sir Nathan."

01

Corpse Reviver

HOLLOW REGALIA

HOLLOW REGALIA

Corpse Reviver

01

Gakuto Mikumo

Illustration by **MIYUU**

YEN ON

NEW YORK

UTSURONARU REGALIA VOL. 1 Corpse Reviver

Gakuto Mikumo

Translation by Sergio Avila Ramirez
Cover art by Miyuu

UTSURONARU REGALIA Vol. 1 Corpse Reviver
©Gakuto Mikumo 2021
Edited by Dengeki Bunko

First published in Japan in 2021 by KADOKAWA CORPORATION, Tokyo. English translation rights arranged with KADOKAWA CORPORATION, Tokyo through TUTTLE-MORI AGENCY, INC., Tokyo.

English translation © 2023 by Yen Press, LLC

Yen On
150 West 30th Street, 19th Floor
New York, NY 10001

Visit us at yenpress.com
facebook.com/yenpress
twitter.com/yenpress
yenpress.tumblr.com
instagram.com/yenpress

First Yen On Edition: March 2023
Edited by Yen On Editorial: Leilah Labossiere, Payton Campbell
Designed by Yen Press Design: Madelaine Norman

Yen On is an imprint of Yen Press, LLC.
The Yen On name and logo are trademarks of Yen Press, LLC.

Library of Congress Cataloging-in-Publication Data
Names: Mikumo, Gakuto, author. | Miyuu, illustrator. | Avila Ramirez, Sergio, translator.
Title: Hollow regalia / Gakuto Mikumo ; illustration by Miyuu ; translated by Sergio Avila Ramirez.
Other titles: Utsuronaru regalia. English
Description: First Yen On edition. | New York, NY : Yen On, 2023- | Contents: v. 1. Corpse reviver—
Identifiers: LCCN 2022048784 | ISBN 9781975352790 (v. 1 ; trade paperback)
Subjects: LCGFT: Apocalyptic fiction. | Monster fiction. | Light novels.
Classification: LCC PZ7.1.M555 Ho 2023 | DDC [Fic]—dc23
LC record available at https://lccn.loc.gov/2022048784

ISBNs: 978-1-9753-5279-0 (paperback)
        978-1-9753-5280-6 (ebook)

10 9 8 7 6 5 4 3 2 1

LSC-C

Printed in the United States of America

Then

the

Japanese

died

out.

Yahiro rolled on the ground, a powerful shock and scorching pain racking his whole body. Fresh blood gushed from his lungs, and the taste of death filled his mouth.

He could hear the searing wind blowing through the gaps of the decayed steel frames of the structure.

It was summer. The fourth one since the disaster.

Not a trace of human life lingered in the ruins of the city. There was nothing but the calls of the cicadas. Only they did not rest as they cried endlessly to announce the twilight.

What a fierce obsession with life. This species full of such vitality. Dreadful destruction had changed the shape of the land, eradicating any and all human inhabitants, and yet the boisterous insects kept on living as though nothing had happened.

It was as moving as it was repugnant.

All these thoughts flooded Yahiro's mind as he stared at the twilight sky visible through the cracked ceiling. A scarlet afterglow charred the heavens. It was this same red sky that brought to mind those four-year-old memories.

On a summer day like this one, crimson rain, thick as mist, had dyed the world the color of flames.

There were collapsed skyscrapers as far as the eye could see. Wreckage and debris. Trains warped and twisted into gray lumps of metal. Fallen bridges and caved-in roads—not even the earth maintained its form. It was like looking at some foreign land.

Rain fell consistently. Rusty-red rain.

Nothing else moved.

Not a single person had survived.

Millions of citizens, wiped out of existence. Devoured so completely that not even corpses remained.

The only one left behind was Yahiro Narusawa—age thirteen, his bloody fists clenched.

"Su...i...!"

His voice rang hollow throughout the silent ruins.

The warmth of his sister's small hand lingered in his own, her young, innocent smile still on his mind. But she was nowhere to be found. There was only the fresh blood that drenched Yahiro's whole body.

"Where are you...Sui...?!"

No voice answered his yells; the quiet wind just increased in intensity.

Yahiro had climbed rubble-strewn stairs to get a better view from a higher vantage point.

It was like a poorly crafted diorama. A ravaged ghost town drenched in crimson rain. Fires burned all over the city and gave the morning sky an evening glow.

The cataclysm cavorted in the sky. A giant shadow that enveloped the whole world. A rainbow-colored monster swimming through the clouds in a spiral, looking down at the ground with contempt.

"Thank goodness...you're alive, Dear Brother."

He heard a clear, cheerful voice.

The soaring monster had pranced behind the girl as she looked down at Yahiro; chills ran along his spine.

Sui Narusawa had smiled softly amid the crimson rain.

"…Or was it that you just could not die?"

It would not leave. He could not get away from that memory, even now. The memory of her clear eyes reflecting the world in ruins and that beautiful, atrocious dragon behind her.

"…Tsk!"

His consciousness faded for just a moment.

Yahiro frantically awoke, irate, and rolled over before jumping back up.

The fangs of the beast grazed the top of his head. The ferocious Moujuu stood three meters tall.

It rushed him with unnecessary momentum and crashed into the concrete. Yahiro used the opportunity to pick his knife back up and regain his footing.

His wound was ridiculously deep. One of his lungs was crushed, and his right shoulder blade was pulverized. His arm was barely connected to his body.

A human's frail body couldn't withstand even the lightest hit from a Moujuu's forelimb. Pain burned endlessly through Yahiro's nerves.

The beast crushed the concrete in its jaws and turned back to him.

The smell of burned sulfur prickled Yahiro's nose.

The Moujuu was shaped like a jet-black dog. The army guys would have gladly named it Black Dog or Hellhound had they found it first, but Yahiro had no interest in naming these things.

Moujuu were just that. Beasts. Monsters that had to be exterminated as soon as they attacked him.

The black Moujuu let out a sulfuric breath as it lowered its body.

It was as large as a bison. As agile and intelligent as a hound. They existed well outside the laws of nature; a single human wasn't enough against their unearthly combat prowess.

Yahiro's watchmen had already escaped or might have even been killed. In any event the guys made no effort to hide their contempt toward the young Japanese man. They would never have helped him, even if they were still alive.

It was nothing short of a miracle that Yahiro could still move with those wounds, and his only weapon was a knife.

No problem, he thought as the corner of his mouth curled up.

He dug the knife into his own wound, coating it in fresh blood.

The black Moujuu growled as it launched itself at him.

Rather than flee, he met the beast head-on.

The two silhouettes collided in the darkness.

The Moujuu tried to dig its giant fangs into Yahiro's left arm, but it could not bite through it. His arm stopped the jaws—capable of biting through concrete—in their tracks. The fresh blood on his skin had hardened like armor.

Yahiro already had the knife in his right hand.

"It's time for revenge!" he called to the bloody knife before stabbing the Moujuu in its side.

The blade was not even fifteen centimeters long—too small for his enormous opponent. Burying it all the way in just barely penetrated its thick skin.

Still, the effect on its body was dramatic.

Cracks ran from the stab wound across its jet-black body. They extended across its entire mass through its blood vessels, the poison inside Yahiro's blood inflicting destruction.

The beast roared in pain. Rage and hate burned in its eyes as it glared at Yahiro.

But its resistance ended there.

Its limbs could no longer support its crumbling body, and it collapsed like a fragile plaster figure.

The Moujuu crumbled into dust as Yahiro watched, emotionless.

He put the knife back into its sheath, then touched his bloody right shoulder.

His crushed lung, his pulverized shoulder, and his torn arm had already regenerated. There was no visible wound. The only remaining evidence of all that had transpired was the blood on his tattered clothes.

That his arm was nearly ripped from his body only accelerated the process, but with or without an arm, regeneration was more than possible.

Yahiro would not die. He could not.

Even if he was to suffer a lethal wound, so long as half his body remained, the curse would not let him die; all his organs would be reconstructed.

This was why only he had made it out of the ruins on that rainy day four years ago.

Yahiro grabbed what he was there for and left the building.

The desolate ruined city spread out under the twilight far toward the horizon.

All the giant half-destroyed towers looked fossilized—steel towers such as the Tokyo Skytree.

It was summer. The fourth summer since the Japanese had gone extinct.

Nevertheless, Yahiro wandered through this city.

HOLLOW
REGALIA

01
Corpse
Reviver

Presented by
GAKUTO MIKUMO

Illustration
MIYUU

Corpse Reviver

1

"Waooon! Hi, everywaon, Iroha Waon here!

"Thanks for tuning in again today. Such nice weather we've had these last few days, huh? We're at almost 32 degrees Celsius out here! Man, that's hot. Remember to stay hydrated!

"...But seriously, it's too hot to be singing and dancing, so today we're having lunch indoors! I'm gonna try my hand at some Japanese cuisine!

"You aren't going to believe this, but I'm actually really good at cooking! No, no, seriously. I'm not lying! Look, you'll see. I'll be making a meat-and-potato dish called *nikujaga* today!"

†

Between the abandoned buildings on the east bank of the Edo River, there was a shady-looking store of mysterious imported goods.

A small figure sat at the back of the shop. It was an old Mexican man wearing gaudy clothing. He puffed on a half-finished cigar as he flipped through the faded pages of a manga, a Japanese comic book magazine.

"I'm back, Ed."

Yahiro entered the store and threw a package on the counter before the manager. It was a box made of paulownia wood, thin and as long as he was tall.

"You're alone, Yahiro? What about the bodyguards the client sent with you?"

Eduardo Valenzuela kept the manga open as he shot Yahiro an irritated glance.

"Bodyguards? Hmph, yeah, like they'd ever look out for me," he answered frankly.

Yahiro produced a couple of silver metal plates from his pocket. Stainless-steel dog tags. He had taken them from the necks of the mercenaries who had escorted him.

"Dead, huh?" Ed stated impassively.

It was nothing out of the ordinary for people to die after entering the 23 Wards. Even less unexpected in this case, considering the mercenaries weren't locals. What was shocking was Yahiro's survival even after years of repeated visits to this danger zone.

"A Moujuu attacked us. Huge black dog. It was near the Senju police station."

"I see."

Ed took note of it and posted it on the map on the wall.

Reliable intel on Moujuu came at a high price—survival depended on it. This information was much more valuable to Ed than the details of the mercenaries' deaths.

"So what about our target?"

"It's right here. Had a hard time finding it, though—it wasn't just lying around at a museum or something." Yahiro pointed at the box.

Ed opened the lid without much care and found a sword sling

containing a single katana. An *uchigatana-koshirae*. A relic that truly belonged in a museum.

"Kuyo Masakane, one of the National Treasures… Looks like the real thing."

Ed smiled in satisfaction after reading the note on the bottom of the box. The calligraphy brushstrokes on it looked like nothing but hieroglyphs to Yahiro.

"How can you even read that? I'm Japanese, and I have no idea what it says."

"How else do you expect me to be in the art business?"

"Yeah. Right. The art business."

Yahiro chuckled at Ed's boasting.

Ed's trade was in getting valuable art pieces from the ruins of Tokyo and selling them off to foreign aesthetes. It was no noble business to be proud of. It was just junk collection, in reality. Looting.

"You complaining?"

"No, so long as you pay me." Yahiro shook his head with an awkward smile.

Yahiro's job was to go into the 23 Wards and salvage the art pieces Ed asked for. He was essentially a looting subcontractor.

He felt no guilt about selling national artwork to foreigners. The country was done for anyway; trying to keep the treasure there was silly.

"Yeah, your compensation. Of course I'll pay."

Ed got a roll of banknotes from the drawer and tossed it over to Yahiro. The dirty dollar bills were many in number, but the total sum wasn't much. Barely $10,000. No need to even count them.

"Wasn't this for fifty grand?"

"Minus the brokerage fee." Ed felt no shame as he replied to Yahiro's protest. "Negotiating with the client. Appraisal of the goods. It all comes at a cost. Intel's never free."

"Still, why do you get a bigger piece of the pie? You're just sitting there reading some stupid manga."

"You call this stupid? No, no. Manga sells for a decent price to the right clients. Look, this one's got the *Solomon's Lore* one-shot from before it got serialized."

"I don't care about that. And first of all, *I* got that magazine, risking *my* life in the 23 Wards," Yahiro said in a low voice.

Ed softly exhaled the smoke and grinned.

"If you've got a problem, then go find your next client elsewhere. Let's see where you find someone willing to employ a Japanese person."

There came a metallic crunching sound from Yahiro's hand; his grip had crushed the steel dog tags. He slammed them on the counter.

"Yikes." Ed shrugged with an exaggerated motion. "You want money? How about you ask a triad for a job? The Chiva Cartel's looking for bodyguards. I'm sure you'd make a killing there."

"*Killing* is what I don't wanna do. Unless you're the target, I guess," Yahiro grumbled.

Ed sighed. "What a bunch of ingrates the Japanese are."

"I'm supposed to be grateful that you're ripping me off?"

Yahiro grabbed the dollar roll in an outrage, then hurled it in his pouch as is.

"...The private military companies of the Kanto area are gathering their resources. That's why the cartel bunch is so on edge. Looks like something big's gonna happen soon in the 23 Wards," Ed told him before he could storm out of the shop.

Yahiro stopped and turned back.

"Something big?"

"I don't know what exactly. But I might tell you if you leave the money here."

"You wish. This has nothing to do with me."

"I sure hope so. Rumor says they're looking for salvagers going in and out of the 23 Wards. Take care, buddy," he said indifferently before going back to reading the manga.

PMCs looking for salvagers… Ed's warning was worth keeping in mind.

Still, he didn't want to thank him. Ed had basically discounted the cost of the intel before paying him. Though he guessed he was a relatively decent guy, being willing to work with a Japanese and whatnot.

Go to hell, old fart, he thought before leaving the store behind.

2

They say it all started with one meteorite.

It was a small rock, barely more than 365 meters in diameter. They called the asteroid Vritra. The astronomers were too optimistic. Vritra, the Demonic Dragon, changed course erratically and entered the atmosphere, broke into a million pieces, and rained down over the Japanese archipelago.

The shock of the meteorite's impact caused an earthquake of magnitude 9.1. A kilometers-long crater formed at the core of the fall, wreaking destruction on the entire nation of Japan.

And the tragedy did not end there.

The Earth's crust became unstable due to the impact, triggering several large-scale volcanic eruptions, including Mount Fuji.

The pyroclastic flow, rocks, and volcanic ash devastated transportation networks across the country.

Afterward, fierce monsters that defied the known laws of biology started appearing left and right. Strange life-forms that looked like creatures from myth and folktales. They were spectral beasts named Moujuu.

They attacked people indiscriminately. Devoured them. Demolished the cities.

Hunting rifles and shotguns were useless against the Moujuu. The police could do nothing. Even the JSDF was powerless. The Japanese government was already in chaos after the meteorite;

they offered no salvation. Half the citizens of Japan died one week after the Moujuu appeared.

The international community did not sit idly on their thumbs as tragedy unfolded. Donations and relief supplies were sent from all around the world, and auxiliary troops were to be deployed imminently.

The news brought courage to the Japanese people. The nation would recover from this disaster, as they had done so many times in the past. No matter how long it took, this land would know peace once more. Unfounded hope budded within the hearts of the people.

It was then that the situation took another turn.

Out of the blue, leaders around the world, heads of state as well as religious figures, gave out the same order, as though in conspiracy.

"Kill the Japanese people." "Annihilate them."

So began the Japanese Hunt. The J-nocide.

A bloody chain reaction spread the world over. Armies invaded Japan without hesitation.

There were many justifications for the J-nocide.

The UN stated that these were desperate measures to prevent a pandemic from a virus found on the meteorite. Some nations proclaimed the Japanese were planning large-scale acts of terrorism due to their critical situation. Many religious figures declared Japan a dirty den of spirits—the Whore of Babylon itself, as described in the Book of Revelation.

The theory that held the most influence among them stated that the Moujuu were biological weapons developed in secret by the Japanese government.

There were people who questioned the statements, but their objections were dismissed. In the end, pandemonium won out, and the world hated, feared, and killed the Japanese.

The country of Japan soon collapsed in the furor, and the few Japanese people abroad were also violently, mercilessly exterminated one by one.

Once the natural disasters brought about by the meteorite fall began to wane, the J-nocide came to an end.

Half a year had gone by since the fall of Vritra.

In that short time, more than 126 million people died.

And the Japanese went extinct.

3

"Waooon! Hi, everywaon, Iroha Waon here!

"Thanks for tuning in today. Now, dear viewers, have you already noticed? I got a new outfit! Just look at this! Woo-wee!

"As you might be able to tell, this outfit's a bit more daring than the last. Geez, I feel practically naked! But hey, this is what summer's all about!

"You see, the last outfit was getting a little tight around the arms; it felt like it'd burst any minute now... N-no, hey! I'm not getting fat! I'm just growing, okay?!"

†

Yahiro crossed the railway bridge of the Joban Line over the Edo River on foot, entering the quarantine zone. His base was in the ruins of the private university near the Kanamachi Station.

More than thirty nations had deployed armies to Japan for the J-nocide. Eight of them still remained, ruling over parts of Japan. However, since the conquered Japanese had died out, population density saw a sharp drop.

The occupying armies stayed in the main ports and cities. Most of the Japanese archipelago was neglected, without government—turned into a lawless land full of international criminals and terrorists.

But there was one place into which none of them dared step foot. The 23 Wards—the metropolitan area of Tokyo. The heart of Japan's politics and economy. The former capital was quarantined for a simple reason: Many, many more Moujuu appeared there compared to elsewhere. And the beasts became fiercer and more dangerous the closer you got to the center of the city.

This was why so many valuable pieces of art and other artifacts remained within the buildings of the city, even four years after the J-nocide.

It was the Moujuu's home, untamed by human hands.

Which was why Yahiro spent the nights there. No burglar would approach him so long as he remained within the 23 Wards.

What if a Moujuu attacked? Then he would just have to kill it. It wasn't so easy when the opponent was a fellow human.

The country had fallen. There was no one left to punish him for the crime of murder. Still, he felt like he would lose his last anchor as a proud Japanese were he to cross that line.

He knew it was mere sentimentality. Complacency. But he felt it wasn't fair for him, who was unable to die, to take another's life. So he refused to kill people. He did so as to not forget his Japanese roots—his human roots.

"Though I guess if you really get down to it, I shouldn't be trespassing and thieving, either."

Forgive me for breaking and entering into an abandoned school, okay?

It didn't feel right to be all alone in the big classrooms, so Yahiro mostly used the tiny labs. He threw his stuff on the sofa he used as a bed and grabbed the cans, chocolates, and mineral water he had in stock for dinner.

Ed could probably get him some beef, fish, or even freshly baked bread, but he dared not ask him for food. He didn't even want to imagine how much he would try to get out of him for it.

Yahiro had chosen this campus as a home because the solar-power station of the building still worked. It wasn't on full capacity, since most of the solar panels were destroyed, but it produced more power than he could use by himself.

He grabbed the modded smartphone he left charging during the day and sneaked into the army's network. He hadn't always been a hacking wizard, but being left all alone in that city, he'd had ample time to learn. He used a specialized tool to get into the network and, through the server of the Canadian Army up in northern Kanto, he connected to a foreign video-streaming site.

He soon found the channel he was looking for.

A pretty girl wearing a wig with animal ears showed up on his phone's screen.

"Waooon! Hi, everywaon, Iroha Waon here!
"Thanks for tuning in today. Sure is chilly at night, huh? And damn, those noisy cicadas! Can you hear me, everyone? Hello?!"

Yahiro's face softened up once he heard her usual cheery greeting.

She had silver hair and green eyes. Wore a bizarre outfit like an anime character. Iroha Waon was an amateur internet streamer. Her videos were mostly about trivial conversation, though she sometimes cooked live or sang and danced.

Her videos were not particularly interesting. There was nothing of note about her, beside the pretty face.

The topics of conversation she chose were nothing controversial, and her cooking was barely average. Her dancing was surprisingly good, but her singing was dreadful.

Her view count was nothing to write home about, either. She got to the three digits only on the rare good day.

However, her videos were something special, invaluable to Yahiro for one simple reason: They were in Japanese.

Iroha Waon was either Japanese herself or with some deep relation to the culture.

She kept on speaking the language of a dead nation. Perhaps only to make herself stand out. That was the most probable reason why. Maybe there was no Iroha Waon; it could be someone else maliciously pretending to be Japanese. But Yahiro did not care.

Just hearing that nostalgic sound, the mere idea of another Japanese person beside him being alive out there somewhere, gave him hope.

"Tonight we're having a Q&A session. Let's look at the first comment! From Yahiron in Tokyo! Thank you for writing all the time!"

"—!"

Yahiro pumped his fist upon hearing her say his name. Yahiron was his handle. She then read his message:

"Yahiron, is it true you live in Tokyo? I mean, I do, too! According to the lore, at least. Would be nice to meet you one day, neighbor... Anyway, let's hear our first question of the nigh—"

Yahiro stared intently at the phone, the screen mere inches from his face, but then he could no longer hear her. A gunshot drowned out the sound coming from the speakers.

"...What?"

* * *

Yahiro looked up, dumbfounded, and immediately grabbed his knife and rushed out of the room. Gunshots kept echoing. They were coming from the courtyard.

"Why would anybody be here?!"

Moujuu didn't use guns, obviously. Someone was in this school. Yahiro naturally assumed someone had inadvertently stepped into the 23 Wards and was being attacked by a Moujuu.

The intruder deserved it for entering the quarantine area; Yahiro had no reason to save them. But he couldn't have someone dying inside his own base. The smell of their blood would attract more Moujuu.

Yahiro kicked the door open–lock was broken–and rushed out to the courtyard. He immediately stood in place, shocked.

"Whoa?!"

A body came flying in his direction, passed by right before his eyes, and crashed into the wall. It was a big man wearing a bulletproof vest. He broke the glass window in a hundred pieces and rolled on the floor, drenched in blood.

"Hey, Yahiro Narusawa!" Someone called his name as he stood there flabbergasted.

It was a young Asian woman. A small girl wearing a sleeveless Chinese blouse. She had black hair with orange highlights in an asymmetric haircut. Looked about Yahiro's age, so around sixteen. She was dressed extremely lightly for someone inside the 23 Wards and had no real weapon in hand. There was no doubt, however, that it was her who had sent the man in the bulletproof vest flying, using a peculiar martial art move similar to aikido.

"Dam...mit...!" The man pointed his submachine gun at the girl.

The expression on her face remained the same, and, before the man could pull the trigger, gunshots echoed from somewhere else. The man let out a voiceless scream as his right hand was blown off.

It was another girl, with the same exact face as the one with orange highlights, who had shot him.

She had the wide eyes of a capricious cat. Handsome, otherworldly features. The two of them looked really similar, even for sisters. In fact, their hairstyles—asymmetrical with one side longer than the other—were the same, only the asymmetrical sides were mirrored. The one differing trait was the color of her highlights: blue.

The blue-haired girl held a gun in each hand. She shot each of them once, so quickly she could not have possibly had time to properly aim, but the shots were precise. Two men fell to their deaths, bullets right between their eyebrows.

"Rosy, I found him! Yahiro Narusawa." The orange-haired girl waved at her double.

Blue-haired "Rosy" put back the guns on the holsters on her thighs and approached them. She showed no enmity toward Yahiro.

"Yahiro Narusawa. You're him, right? Wow, you're so young... And that look in your eyes aside, you've got a pretty cute face. I smell fun." The orange-haired girl sniffed him.

Yahiro kept a hand on his knife, ready to unsheathe at any moment, as he stared back at her in silence.

He thought hard. What were they doing there? Why did they know his name? What did they want? Were they on his side or not?

"Sorry for the intrusion, Yahiro Narusawa," said the blue-haired girl.

Despite the identical faces, the impression he got from their eyes was quite the opposite. The orange-haired girl looked like a curious cat, while the blue-haired girl seemed entirely emotionless.

"Right... Who are these guys?" he asked.

"Agents hired by some private military company. They were following us. I suppose they were trying to stop us from getting in contact with you."

"Why would a PMC do that...?" he said with a frown. Ed's warning came to mind.

This could not be unrelated to the rumor about them investigating salvagers. It even made him wonder whether that man had known this would happen from the very beginning.

"Well..." The blue-haired girl tried to answer, but she suddenly narrowed her eyes and unsheathed her gun. She aimed at the man in the bulletproof vest she had sent flying at the start of their encounter.

"Yahiro...Narusawaaa...!" the man roared as he glared at him with bloodshot eyes.

His muscles bulged in an unusual way, immediately blowing away his bulletproof vest.

"You were still conscious?"

The blue-haired girl pulled the trigger, mercilessly burying a bullet in his forehead. Her shot was mechanically precise. The 9mm bullet pierced his skull, lethally damaging his brain...or at least it should have.

"Oooooh!"

The man did not stop moving. His entire body was drenched in his own blood as he howled, joy on his face. His eyes shone brightly as he glared at Yahiro.

"What's...going on...?"

Yahiro unsheathed his knife on instinct. The man looked like an entity full of deep-rooted loathing, like a Moujuu...or worse.

"He took the F-med!"

The blue-haired girl's eyes locked onto the man's neck. A cylinder two inches in diameter was injected into his left carotid artery like a syringe. The liquid inside it was red like wine, most of it already flowing into the man's body, granting him supernatural vitality.

"Rosy, get down! It's a Fafnir soldier!"

The orange-haired girl kicked off from the ground and leaped toward the man. Her small body deftly put his arm in a hold, her whole weight bending it in an unnatural direction. A crack echoed, but the man paid no attention to his broken arm and swung it to send her flying.

"Giuli?!" the blue-haired girl screamed.

"That was spooky!" The orange-haired girl spun in the air and landed on a wall like a cat. She jumped to the ground like it was nothing, then distanced herself from the bloody man.

He wasn't even looking at them; he held his broken left arm high above his head, and, with a cracking sound, it started distorting. Solid scales covered his skin, thorns jutting out of it like knives—exactly like a giant reptile's forelimb.

"Yes... This power...! I could easily kill Moujuu with this power!" The man bared his teeth in a twisted smile, clenching his clawed fist. Then, suddenly, his glare turned to Yahiro.

"You... What is that smell?!"

The man bellowed in a hoarse, hard-to-make-out voice before jumping right at him. Yahiro's reflexes couldn't keep up with his supernatural strength.

The man thrust his left hand, broadly slashing the left side of Yahiro's chest with his claws. But then he started shrieking in pain as Yahiro's blood splattered on him.

"Oh, so you're the Lazarus... *Lazarus!!*"

"Guh?!"

The man's claws slashed at him yet again, but Yahiro stopped the attack with his bare arm. He clenched his muscles to keep the claws buried, preventing further action from the opponent. Then he stabbed his knife, drenched in his own blood, into the man's shoulder.

"Gwoooh!" The man cried out like a beast.

He swung his bulging and swollen left arm around to try and force his claws out. What followed, though, was unpredictable even to Yahiro: The man's arm snapped off his shoulder with a dry sound like a twig cracking.

""Wha...?!"" both of them exclaimed in unison.

Recoiling, each of them stumbled backward. Yahiro rolled on the ground before hurriedly standing back up and reflexively holding up his knife, but then he gasped in shock.

"This... This is nooo...thi...!"

The man's body was melting. His body had swollen up three times bigger and was turning slimy black, like pus.

He could not control the chaotic multiplication of his body's cells. He no longer looked human. Soon enough, it went beyond its physical limitations and burst like a balloon, splattering rotten fluid all over.

It was a grand death. A theatrical collapse.

Yahiro could do nothing but stand and watch, aghast.

Silence returned to the college ruins.

Yahiro breathed out softly after hearing movement behind him. He returned his chipped knife to its sheath and stood up. He locked eyes with the twins.

"Care to explain?" he asked, suppressing his irritation.

"Yes, of course. We came here for exactly that," the blue-haired girl answered with a pretty smile and empty eyes.

4

"Wait, Giuli. We must first check that there are no traps."

"It's fine. Look, the door's not even locked. We're coming in!" The orange-haired girl entered the lab before Yahiro could even try to stop her. Her eyes rounded in amazement at the sight of the clearly inhabited room. "Hey, Yahiro Narusawa, can I take this? It looks yummy."

She grabbed a can of food with keen interest. Yakitori with soy sauce—a rare sight for non-Japanese people, perhaps.

"Do whatever you want," he replied before handing her a camping fork. "And just call me Yahiro, okay? No need to say my last name every time."

"Okay. Then you call me Giuli. Rosy's Rosy."

"...Call me Rosé at the very least, please." The blue-haired girl sighed in reluctance.

Giuli and Rosé. He had figured out they were sisters just from this short exchange.

"We're from Galerie Berith. Merchants," Rosé told him.

Yahiro's shoulders remained tense as he frowned slightly. *Galerie* was the French pronunciation for *gallery*, if he recalled correctly.

"Galerie... So you're art dealers?"

"Indeed. Officially, at any rate."

"Officially...eh?" Yahiro smiled awkwardly. *Guess they're frank, if nothing else.*

So they were in the same business as Ed. The shady business of selling off the art pieces and antiques left behind in Japan. It made sense why they had crossed into the 23 Wards to meet him, then.

"I am Rosetta Berith. My cute little twin over there is Giulietta. We came here to make you a salvage request."

"Cute little twin, huh?" *That supposed to be a roundabout way to say you're cute, too?* "So you want me to go get some goods."

"Yes."

"Why me, though? There're other salvagers out there, right?"

"One of the reasons why is because you are a surviving Japanese person. We believe we should get help from one in order to get the goods in question."

"Do I gotta solve a Japanese riddle or something?" He narrowed his eyes in suspicion.

The nation of Japan had fallen the moment most of its citizens died off. There was no one to keep its culture and language alive, and all of its leftover assets were flowing out abroad. The only remaining value of the Japanese people was as a piece of history.

If there was something only Yahiro could help with, it would be to solve some sort of special code only a Japanese person would understand.

"Oooh...so you're good at riddles? That's amazing!" Orange-haired Giulietta's eyes lit up.

Yahiro felt awkward at that reaction.

"I'm not good or anything. I was just asking."

"Oh... Pfft. Boring." She puffed her cheeks like a sulking child.

Yahiro ignored her and turned to look at Rosé. "So what's the other reason for hiring me?"

Rosé's lips curled up mischievously. Her eyes were fixed on the slash on Yahiro's shirt, where the monstrous guy who took the F-med had attacked him. The wound beneath it had entirely vanished.

"Because you are immortal... The Lazarus, Yahiro Narusawa."

"...?!" Yahiro gasped in shock. He immediately tried to pretend to be unfazed, but it was obviously too late.

He had no reliable partners or support. His immortal body was his only weapon. The enemy always let their guard down the moment they thought he was dead—and that was his chance for retaliation. He had to outsmart his foes, who were superior in strength, to survive, whether they were Moujuu or human. But the trick didn't quite work if the secret was out.

He had concealed the truth about himself up to this moment. Not even Ed, whom he had known for a long time already, knew about it. And even if silly rumors about an immortal, cursed Japanese made the rounds, no one seriously believed them.

Rosé's tone, however, made it clear she was sure of it.

"Laza...rus?" Yahiro repeated. He hadn't heard the word before and was strangely intrigued by it.

"Germanic mythology tells the story of the hero Siegfried, who killed a dragon and bathed in its blood to obtain an immortal body... I wonder how you became the Lazarus." Rosé tilted her head sideways.

Yahiro felt his expression freeze upon hearing them casually mention the dragon slayer's legend.

Rosé narrowed her eyes, gazing at him with glee.

"Do tell, Yahiro."

5

"This is so tasty. It would go great with some liquor. Do you have wine here somewhere?" Giuli broke the awkward silence while still chewing a bite of yakitori.

"I do not. Aren't you too young for that? Just drink some water." He hurled a bottle of mineral water at her.

He'd gotten that from the university's emergency stock. There was more than he could ever drink left over.

Giuli grabbed it without complaint; then she inexplicably puffed up her chest in pride.

"Oh, you got that wrong. In my country, you can drink from age sixteen."

"And where is that, exactly?"

"Where was it, again, Rosy?"

"Belgium. Though that is only our official citizenship, for convenience's sake," Rosé answered blandly.

She always appeared expressionless, but her gaze turned soft whenever she looked at her sister and responded to all her stupid questions without ever seeming annoyed.

"So what's Lazarus mean?" Yahiro asked Rosé, anxiety leaving his face.

"It's the name we use to refer to those who can come back from the dead. It's got no special meaning, but it comes from the Bible's Gospel of John... Ever read the New Testament?"

"Never."

"Me neither." Giuli shook her head and also replied in the negative.

Rosé wasn't expecting her older sister to answer; her expression soured, but soon enough she sighed in amusement.

"Oh, so you're not denying you're immortal."

"You're here because you know I am, aren'tcha?" Yahiro replied with a grimace.

He had no idea why, but Rosé was already absolutely sure he was immortal. He figured it would be pointless to try to feign ignorance.

"Bummer. If only you had denied it, I would've gotten to slash your throat open to check whether you were lying or not." Giuli, still munching delightedly on yakitori, pointed the fork at him.

Chills went down his spine. He couldn't react even to that simple motion until it was over. He would have died at least once had she been serious. She was certain of this, even, which was why she said it—a twisted way of telling him she wasn't interested in actually doing it. Or at least that was how he took it.

"Who told you about me?" he asked Rosé again.

"The mercenaries watching over you on your mission to retrieve Kuyo Masakane were our underlings," she replied in a monotone.

Yahiro nodded slightly, unable to hide his discomfort entirely. He felt sorry about letting them die, despite the two watchmen being nasty cretins who looked down on him for being Japanese.

"So you were our clients?"

"The drones we sent with them recorded your battle against the Moujuu. You received lethal wounds that should have killed you instantly, but then your body quickly regenerated." Rosé observed his reactions intently.

Giuli, on the other hand, stared at the now-empty yakitori can before clearing her throat.

"We were looking forward to meeting you. We'd heard about a cursed Japanese salvager who always came back from the deadliest of places."

"And what, exactly, do you want this cursed Japanese guy to get for you?" he asked bluntly.

Rosé's reply was short: "The Kushinada."

"...Kushinada?"

"Ever read the Kojiki?"

"The whole country went under before I could finish compulsory education, okay? Don't expect me to be very cultured." Yahiro looked away grouchily.

The Bible was one thing, but hearing that these foreigners knew more about Japanese culture than he did was nothing short of humiliating.

The J-nocide began four years back, when he was still a first-year middle school student.

He had survived on his own ever since. There was no way to even hope for a decent education. There were many books left behind for self-study, but he had to prioritize what had more practical use, such as foreign languages and electrical engineering. He hadn't gotten around to studying history yet.

"I know the name, at least. It's a goddess of Japanese mythology, right?"

"Correct. She was the medium chosen as a sacrifice to Yamata no Orochi, the Eight-Headed Dragon."

"A sacrifice...for a dragon..." Yahiro's cheeks tensed up unconsciously.

Rosé's bangs swayed as she nodded ominously.

"Do you know why the 23 Wards have been quarantined?"

"Because they're full of Moujuu?"

"Yes. Moujuu have a ninety-times higher chance of emerging here than elsewhere. Kyoto and Nara are considered high-ratio spots as well, but the 23 Wards still have a ratio ten times higher than those."

"And many of them are strong to boot. You'd hear about entire armored corps falling against a single Moujuu a long time ago," Giuli added with a smile.

A long time ago...meant barely three, four years back. Troops from all over the world rushed to Tokyo to gain control of the former capital, and they all suffered great losses. As a result, the 23 Wards were sealed off and labeled a quarantine zone that belonged to no group.

"You knew all that and still came here? You've got guts; I'll give you that." Yahiro sighed.

Two small girls stepping all alone into the Moujuu-infested 23 Wards. The height of insanity.

Giuli seemed pleased, however: "Hear that, Rosy?! He praised us!"

"I was being sarcastic!"

"Fair enough. Even here near the border of the 23 Wards is dangerous enough compared to other places, but yes, we judged that we'd be able to make our way through." Rosé answered calmly as Yahiro frowned at them being unfazed by his comment. "Still, we don't plan on going any farther than this. The Moujuu become more and more dangerous the closer you get to the center, don't they?"

"They do." Yahiro nodded bluntly.

Although within the 23 Wards, around the areas of Tama, Suginami, Nerima, or even Setagaya and Ohta, which faced Kanagawa prefecture, there were relatively few Moujuu. The emergence ratio was barely five or six times that of the so-called buffer area, which included South Saitama and West Chiba.

Meanwhile, closer to the city's center, you had emergence ratios a hundred times higher.

Not even a salvager like Yahiro dared approach the area of the Yamanote Line. No matter how good the pay. Rumor had it that no one had seen Tokyo Station and made it back alive—and this was all too real. Yahiro understood it very well.

"That is why we're here with you, Yahiro Narusawa."

"Excuse me?"

"We've identified a group of Moujuu banding together around the ruins of the Tokyo Dome, in what used to be Bunkyo. Various kinds gather there, and they appear to be expanding their domain."

"Moujuu…are forming herds? And you're saying different types of them are living together?" *That can't be.* He shook his head.

Moujuu were unclassifiable monsters, detached from the laws of nature's kingdoms. Except for those who appeared as colonies, Moujuu of the same kind rarely emerged at the same time. He had never heard of them establishing groups on a large scale, let alone doing so in mixed species.

Rosé, however, kept on talking calmly. "We believe they have a leader."

"Is Kushinada the name of that leader?"

"Yes," the blue-haired girl affirmed.

Yahiro pressed his lips together. If what Rosé said was right, then this Kushinada specimen would certainly have immense value. No wonder these so-called merchants showed interest in it.

"We don't know how Kushinada is taming the Moujuu, but if we can figure that out, it could lead to developing the technology for it."

"A way for humanity to control the Moujuu? Sounds like that'd make a killing," he said sarcastically.

Rosé did not deny it.

"On the other hand, if we let Kushinada run free, the Moujuu herd under its control could become a threat to humanity."

"A threat to humanity, huh…?" He huffed. Didn't sound like an improbability.

The Moujuu were dangerous monsters, and the only reason why they hadn't yet become a danger to the rest of humanity was because they only emerged independently. So long as no one intruded on their territory, they generally wouldn't actively attack humans. Which was why the UN had sealed off the 23 Wards and was satisfied with that one precaution.

Things changed if they were grouping up, though. Their numbers would only increase as long as they didn't fight among themselves.

No one had yet confirmed that Moujuu ate like other living creatures. But no one could guarantee they would never run out of food, either. And obviously, if the food they had within the 23 Wards ran out, they would look for it outside. The chances of them being able to cross the seas and attack other countries wasn't zero, either.

Capturing Kushinada before that happened was reasonable enough. Even more so when they knew its powers would rake in the dough.

"You're asking me to go retrieve this Kushinada?" Yahiro asked, indisputably wary.

"Can you?" Giuli raised her head with great expectations.

"'Course not. There's already enough wild Moujuu just after the former Yamanote Line. You want me to go against *all of them*?"

"Right." The elder twin shrugged.

"We don't intend to make you go alone." The younger twin spoke seriously. "Operation: Kushinada Hunt will take place in two days, led by the military corporation Raimat. Galerie Berith plans on joining, so—"

"We want you to show us the way." Giuli interrupted Rosé with an impish grin.

"You want me to be a tour guide?" Yahiro furrowed his brow. Showing the way wasn't a salvager's job. Surely they could use GPS or drones; what was the need for a guide?

Rosé saw through his doubts and shook her head.

"Capturing Kushinada will be a joint operation among four PMCs hired by Raimat. The idea is we should cooperate, but each troop will be acting independently."

"First come, first served, pretty much." Giuli's big, catlike eyes shone bright with competition.

The participants were employees and contractors for private military companies; despite it being a joint operation, each of them would naturally prioritize their own interests. One could already foresee them trying to outwit one another.

"You have experience entering the 23 Wards. I think you should know a safe route where we would come across the least Moujuu. And you also know about their nature and weak points. We want you to share that knowledge with us and guide us to the Kushinada's territory. Faster than any other group." Rosé finally revealed their true aim.

On top of his achievements as a salvager, Yahiro, as a Japanese citizen, would know the land of Tokyo from before the J-nocide. He could make full use of the signs written in Japanese and other details foreigners might look over. There was no one better for the job.

This also explained why Rosé and Giuli had been attacked by PMC mercenaries, called operators, when they met. A competing firm didn't like Galerie Berith trying to gain an advantage in the operation.

Had the girls never come, perhaps their competitors would have killed Yahiro without him knowing why. Still...

"Sorry, but no. I can't bear responsibility for other people's lives." He declined right away. "You should understand why, seeing as the guys today were your employees. I just happen to be hard to kill; I'm not strong enough to protect other people from the Moujuu. I can't promise I could get you all safely to the center of the 23 Wards."

"Don't worry about the two who died today. It is their own failing for ignoring your instructions and underestimating the Moujuu," Rosé said, monotone.

Even though her intention was to absolve him of guilt, he felt her response to be too apathetic and heartless.

Giuli then tried to cover for her sister, smiling awkwardly as she rested her head on her hand.

"We told them they didn't need to follow you so closely... They got greedy after finding out about the treasure."

"And you need not worry about our survival. You can even run away by yourself if danger arises. But you should know that, in case you don't agree to guide us, then there is no doubt our chances will drop considerably." Rosé spoke as though it wasn't her own life she was talking about.

Yahiro was at a loss for words.

The blue-haired girl spoke the truth. He wasn't strong enough to protect them from the Moujuu, but he could show them a safer route. That would bring their chances of survival up, even if only slightly.

That did not change the fact that their plan was reckless, however. What was the point in doubling or tripling their chances of survival when they were one in a hundred thousand to begin with?

"I don't care what you say; I can't take up a job that risky."

Yahiro stood his ground, hoping they would give up on this Kushinada operation.

He did not expect what Rosé would say next.

"Even if your reward was intel on Sui Narusawa?"

"What...did you just say?"

Yahiro felt as though the blood in his whole body started flowing backward. His throat tightened, and his lungs forgot how to work. His brain froze up at the sound of that name—a name he hadn't forgotten for a single day since that fateful occurrence four years ago.

"I heard the reason why you haven't left the 23 Wards is because you are looking for your baby sister. That most of the money you make as a salvager is spent gathering information on her whereabouts."

"You know where Sui is?" He drew nearer to Rosé.

She shook her head softly. "Maybe I do. Maybe I don't."

"Tell me!" Yahiro reached out to grab her by the collar, but immediately his view of her icy grin turned upside down as severe pain hit his shoulder. "–?!"

"You can't do that, Yahiro. You've gotta lead us if you wanna know." Giuli giggled from above him, and he felt the hard press of the floor against his head.

He could not tell what had happened, other than the fact that Giuli was now pinning him to the floor.

"Let...go!"

Yahiro struggled to let himself out of her grip, but she only pushed down harder on his right shoulder. How was she hiding this much power in that tiny body? It felt like resisting only made her stronger.

"Huh, Rosy's right. The Lazarus's power only activates when you're wounded. Dislocation doesn't entail loss, so you're not regenerating."

"You...asshole...!"

"Hey! Watch your hands! Rosy, are you seeing this? He's totally grabbing my boobs!"

"You're the one holding my hand to your chest!" He protested the slander.

She had his arm in a hold from behind, easily restraining his right arm against her chest. The softness was unmistakable to him even through the pain; he had to be careful about making any move.

"Let it slide this once, Giuli. I am sure this moment must be the happiest in his entire life," Rosé said in an annoyed tone.

The only clear difference between the identical twins was, in fact, breast size.

Giuli was quite well-endowed despite her small frame, while Rosé's bosom was perfectly flat. Perhaps therein lay the reason why her glare turned more hostile after the subject was brought up. Absolutely unfair, however, for Yahiro to be on the receiving end of it.

"This should tell you that there is no need to worry about our safety." Rosé sighed while gesturing to her sister to let him go.

The weight on his back eased. Freed, Yahiro stood, holding his right shoulder, while Giuli unapologetically giggled her way to the sofa.

Giuli was certainly a better fighter than him; he had to give her credit. There was no need for him to try to protect them, and they did not want his protection in the first place.

"So will you guide us to the Kushinada's den?" Rosé asked.

Yahiro returned the glare, then asked: "Do you...really have intel on Sui?"

"Yes."

"If you're lying, I will dedicate my life to making you pay."

"That's quite the threat to make while knowing you're the Lazarus, huh?"

Rosé smiled, not a trace of fear on her face. She then took a photograph out of her chest pocket and threw it at Yahiro.

"What's this?" He grabbed it right before it touched the floor.

It was a printout of a photo taken by a hidden camera.

"Consider this your advance payment. Not a clear picture, but still."

Rosé didn't sound intent on explaining any more.

Yahiro turned it around to see the picture. It had a lot of grain, perhaps taken in a dark place. It showed a medical stretcher in an underground room, no windows. It had a sinister design to it, like a coffin, and on it was a girl, restrained by silver chains and connected to countless tubes. A sleeping girl, like a doll or a corpse—Asian.

Yahiro knew that girl.

"Sui...," he muttered.

His eyes widened in shock, he intently scrutinized the photo. It wasn't dated, but even then, he knew this was a recent picture, no older than a year.

"Your sister...Sui Narusawa is alive. For now." Rosé spoke dispassionately.

Yahiro did not answer; he could only stare at his sister's picture, aghast.

1

"Waooon! Hi, everywaon, Iroha Waon here!

"Thanks for tuning in today. The sky's always clear here at this time. It's hot today as usual, even so early in the morning.

"But today's a special day! It's my seventeenth birthday! Yaaay! Clap, clap, clap! Happy birthday, me! So I'm gonna be baking my own cake today! Well, not a cake, per se, but a cupcake! I got pancake mix here for it!"

†

Operation: Kushinada Hunt began by gathering the troops at the Arakawa Riverside, near the ruins of the Kawaguchi Station. They had to cross the Shin-Arakawa Bridge, which still stood after the J-nocide, and enter the 23 Wards through what once was the Kita Ward. They would then take the National Route 123 to Hakusan Avenue.

Galerie Berith was an arts dealer in name only—their true business was in arms. They called themselves a galerie only out of convenience for the transportation of weaponry and money across national borders. They had their own private military company supposedly to protect the artwork.

The place was chock-full of soft-skinned gun trucks and armored personnel carriers by the time Yahiro arrived. Sharply contrasting with the menacing environment, a pretty girl stood in the middle of it all. The girl with the orange highlights jumped and waved at him.

"He's here! Yahiro, over here!"

Everyone turned around to look at him upon hearing Giulietta Berith's shouting.

Yahiro's expression soured, and he approached her reluctantly.

Giuli was surrounded by the Galerie's operators. They weren't soldiers in the strict sense of the word—calling them contractors would be more accurate. PMC employees were not allowed to use camouflaged military clothing, so they wore their own unique uniform: a sort of hiking hoodie.

The uniform's main color was white and yellow—needlessly stylish for their purpose. It was made of a special material that stayed cool in the middle of summer—breathable while still waterproof. It was also bulletproof and had power-suit functionality in order to sustain the extra weight of those added features. They were worth thousands of dollars.

A showy, costly, and highly functional uniform. Each detail irritated Yahiro more than the last. But what annoyed him the most was the fact that they made him wear one.

"Looks like it fits you well," Rosé said with an unfriendly look on her face as she got off the carrier.

She was wearing the same uniform, but the particulars were a tad different. The bottom was a miniskirt with a slit, and she was exposing more of her shoulders and hips. Perhaps she, like Giuli, prioritized mobility over defense. Or maybe she simply felt hot with all that covered.

"The size's not bad, but it's too heavy," Yahiro grumbled, placing a hand on his chest.

The bulletproof plate, though comparatively lightweight due to the innovative material, was still heavy enough to hinder mobility.

"It has powered assistance. Just boot it up, and you should no longer feel the weight."

"It doesn't change the fact that I'm holding extra weight. And I don't need this much protection."

Gunshots were no threat to the Lazarus boy, and bulletproof plates held no significance against Moujuu. The weight was nothing but a hindrance.

"You can take it off once we enter the 23 Wards, but I think you should keep it on until then. You're more famous than you realize."

Rosé spoke in riddles, and Yahiro couldn't decipher them. Then someone pulled his arm hard before he could ask for clarification.

"Yahiro, Yahiro, take this."

Giuli clung to him as she pushed a bundle, about as thick as a chocolate bar, to his chest. The wrapper enveloping it was that of a luxury confectionery.

"What's this?"

"Some candy. Eat it if you get hungry."

"Well, I hope I get time to think about eating today."

It was small enough to not be a nuisance to carry, so he had no reason to refuse it. He put it in his thigh bag.

Yahiro kept his guard up all the while. He didn't know the twins' rank in the Galerie Berith organization, but he couldn't imagine the operators would welcome with open arms the outsider they had brought. His own life hadn't been peaceful enough for him to be so trusting.

He was anticipating just a bit of harassment but had to be prepared for the worst, such as a bullet to the head out of the blue. No amount of caution was excessive.

"Hey, Japanese boy. So you're the guy the Princess and the Lady brought."

One of the operators spoke to him in casual English, a cheeky look in his eyes. The young white man had his blond hair styled in a Mohawk.

Then he extended his right hand to Yahiro, offering a handshake. He grinned like a playful brat.

"I'm Josh. Josh Keegan. This big gal over here is Paola Resente."

"...I'm not big... You're just short...," the tan-skinned woman replied.

"I'm not short!" Josh objected.

He was relatively short for a white man, while Paola was as tall as a pro model. Their difference in height was staggering.

"You must be Yahiro. I'm Yang Wei. We three are the team leaders of the special forces that will be heading into the 23 Wards as of today. Nice to meet you." A good-looking Asian man asked him for a handshake last.

He seemed older than Josh and Paola but still under thirty. All the other operators also looked about his age. The average age of the troop was far younger than Yahiro had expected.

"...I'll work as hard as the pay merits. Don't expect any more," Yahiro replied awkwardly.

There was something about Wei's friendly smile that didn't sit right with him.

The Japanese became the target of the world's hatred when the J-nocide began, and even after it ended, the contempt and mockery did not. People would gladly use Yahiro as a salvager, but no one considered him their equal.

Being on the receiving end of friendliness all of a sudden left him feeling confused. It was only then that he understood how easy it was to interact with the capricious Giuli and bossy Rosé.

"I see. Either way, Yahiro, there is something you must know before we start. It's important."

Josh's face became serious all of a sudden. He led him somewhere out of Rosé's line of sight.

Here it comes, I guess. The hazing. He expected to get punched in the face to show him who's boss. The usual. What happened in reality, however, he could have never imagined.

"Listen, Yahiro. Don't you go falling for the Princess, okay?"

"…What? Princess? You mean…Giuli?"

"Yes. I mean, if you want to fall in love with her, you do you, but don't lay a finger on her. Got that?"

"Okay…" It was so out there that it took him a second to comprehend.

Giuli was "the Princess." Rosé was "the Lady." At least in Josh's head. Yahiro got the gist of it, but he didn't understand why he was warning him, exactly.

"Everyone in the Galerie is a Giuli fan. Show her the slightest disrespect, and everyone here will turn on you. Expect a bullet to the back if that happens."

"Don't worry… Only Rosé would ever do that…," Paola added, a serious look on her face.

Wei nodded.

Yahiro was speechless. He felt dizzy from the sheer idiocy of the idea. What was this, an idol's fan club? Surely no PMC operator would be so stupid as to choose where to work for such a reason. The most baffling part of this, though, was that Rosé was somehow the leader. Her love for her twin sister was more serious than he initially thought.

The fact that the team leaders were warning him about it had to mean something similar had happened once before, too. *It's incredible this organization can even function properly.*

2

The operation as discussed in the meeting was extremely simple.

They had to reach the Kushinada's den before any other PMC, find it, and capture it. That's it. There was no point in laying out any details anyway, since they would have to act according to the Moujuu's movements once they were inside the 23 Wards.

"The Galerie has gathered two squads, a total of twenty-four people, in order to capture the Kushinada. Half of them will be waiting outside the 23 Wards as logistical support; only one squad will enter," Rosé calmly explained under a tent on the riverside.

"Twelve people… That's too many." Yahiro grimaced.

The more people in one place, the easier it was for a Moujuu to notice them. One squad of these special forces was too large to reach the city center unnoticed. And yet, it hardly felt like enough to capture the Kushinada. Yahiro immediately felt like quitting.

"Fifteen, actually, counting you and us," Rosé corrected him.

Yahiro gazed at the twins, a shocked look on his face. Giuli, incomprehensibly, made peace signs with both hands. *I'm not staring at you in admiration.*

"You're gonna go, too?"

"Of course. You know how the parents normally follow from afar when they send the child on their first errand? It's like that."

"How, exactly?! You saying you're my parents now?!"

"…Are you rebelling? Geez. Teens, huh?" Rosé kept a straight face.

"Pooor baaaby. It's gonna be aww wight. Mommy's hewe." Giuli patted his head.

They actually didn't look like they were joking; Yahiro gave up on objecting further. There was a more pressing matter to discuss.

"So, what's this Kushinada like? Sounds like you know where it lives, but how are we supposed to tell it apart from the other Moujuu?"

"We'll know as soon as we see it."

"How can you be so sure?" He glanced at Rosé with suspicion.

She did not respond and glanced behind Yahiro. A big, wheeled, armored vehicle was just arriving at the riverside. It was a command communication vehicle, with a big antenna on the back. It was marked with the logo of a different PMC.

Armed operators got off the vehicle as soon as it stopped. In order to differentiate themselves from the army personnel, their uniforms were pompous, and reminiscent of medieval knights.

A man with an even more extravagant uniform than the others calmly led the group over to the tent. He was young and beautiful, like something out of a painting. He was tall and appeared to be in his late twenties.

"Ladies and gentlemen of Galerie Berith, excuse us for intruding before the operation begins. We've brought here our sponsor, the chairman of Raimat International. Please show your gratitude to the count's consideration, Galerie guards."

The man spoke in a polite but cocky tone, with the trademark snobbish accent of the bourgeoisie.

"Who the hell are you?" Josh was the first to react; he could not hide his irritation.

"Wait, Josh. That's Firman La Hire, commander in chief of RMS." Wei hurriedly stopped him before he could punch the man.

Yahiro furrowed his brow in silence. He wasn't really in the know, but he had heard of the RMS name. Raimat Military Securika–a PMC owned by one of the world's top arms manufacturers, Raimat International.

They were one of the first to be deployed during the J-nocide, and even today, they worked in many of its cities, transporting goods and maintaining public order. One of the corporations that profited the most out of the J-nocide.

Yahiro had already heard it was Raimat International that planned Operation: Kushinada Hunt. Obviously RMS, their subsidiary, would participate.

"Major, we owe Galerie Berith for joining us in this important operation. Treat them with respect."

"Pardon me, Count." The blond guy straightened before stepping back.

In his place appeared a gray-haired man in a suit. His energetic poise did not match his age—which was well beyond seventy. He had a soft smile on his face, but his eyes were sharp. He was the kind of man Yahiro did not like in the least. The kind who would never dirty his own hands with another person's blood but would easily sign a document that ordered the deaths of millions.

"...Count?"

"Count Hector Raimat, chief executive officer of Raimat International," Rosé replied to Yahiro's involuntary mumble.

The count turned to look at Rosé and bowed cheerfully.

"Ciao, Signorina Berith. I thank you once again for your help with this operation."

"Thank you for coming all the way here to greet us, Count. We are looking forward to working with you today."

Giuli put on a fake smile in silence while Rosé responded politely.

"Oh, no, the pleasure is mine. It is an honor to be able to hire the renowned Berith family." He nodded gracefully.

Then the low humming of an engine echoed. A group of armored flying vehicles was crossing the Shin-Arakawa Bridge that acted as the 23 Wards border. Add that to the wheeled tanks and personnel carriers and there were more than twenty vehicles. Enough to make up a company.

"What is that?"

"That is Ranga Patna's armored corps." The count answered Rosé's question.

Yahiro wasn't imagining the contempt he felt from the man's tone of voice.

"They boasted about gathering a dozen infantry fighting vehicles, the foolish lot. Do they not realize the sound of the engines would only attract the Moujuu?"

"And you still let them go in like that?" Yahiro asked in a critical tone.

The count glanced at him with deep interest, clearly surprised at his worrying about other people's lives.

"Their attracting all the Moujuu will mean we will be safer on the way to our destination. That's simply their job in this joint operation," Rosé explained.

Yahiro grimaced in silence. He finally realized why Raimat, despite their immense numbers, had proposed a joint operation. He planned on using the other PMCs as stepping stones. Galerie was well aware of this and planned on outwitting him. Sly fox versus fox. It was nothing but a wicked game, using people's lives as betting chips.

"As sharp as always, Signorina Berith." The count nodded in satisfaction; he kept on smiling even as he was aware that they knew his true intentions. "And here you have a small troop of elite; I would expect no less of Galerie Berith. I also heard you hired your own guide." He glanced at Yahiro.

He'd known about him from the very beginning. Yahiro then realized that, in fact, he had come all the way there to meet him. However, he didn't understand why he would show such interest in him.

The count continued to stare at him intently as he asked, "I had heard rumors of a cursed Japanese surviving and going in and out of the 23 Wards as a salvager... Major, wouldn't you like to test him?"

"I most certainly would, Count." Firman lifted his right hand, holding a gun. Old, automatic, and engraved with a tacky design. "Excuse me, young man."

"—?!"

An intense shock to his chest sent Yahiro flying backward. It was only after he fell that he heard the gunshots and realized what had happened.

"Yahiro?!"

"La Hire, you bastard!"

Paola and Josh moved right away. She drew her own pistol and pointed it at the RMS operators, while Josh ran up to punch Firman.

Firman raised both hands in a gesture of surrender and easily dodged Josh's attack. He looked at Yahiro on the ground and sighed heavily in disappointment.

"Hah... Immortality? Yeah right. Looks like the cat is out of the bag."

"What?!"

"Josh, wait." Rosé stopped him.

Josh, surprised by her order, froze like a hound scolded by its owner.

Yahiro sighed as he pushed himself up from the pebbled ground. From his chest fell the bent ceramic bulletproof plate that was part of his uniform.

"You wouldn't need this cheap trickery if you truly were immortal. I apologize for scaring you." The count closed his eyes and shook his head with undisguised chagrin.

Yahiro shrugged silently. He didn't enjoy what had just happened, but there was no point in complaining about it. They were his clients, after all.

"Bill Raimat for the plate we ruined. Good-bye," the count said before turning around.

His operators followed him back to the armored vehicle. His imperious strides conveyed that he had nothing left to discuss.

"Wow… That came out of nowhere. You okay, Yahiro? Are your pants dry?" Giuli asked cheerfully as she crouched down beside him.

"Yes, thank you very much," he replied grumpily as he sat up sluggishly.

Three bullet holes marked his uniform, all within four inches of his heart. Firman's quick-fire skill was nothing short of impressive. Even with the bulletproofing, the shock of that would be enough to knock out a regular human. Yahiro didn't stand up immediately because he realized that.

"So this is why you made me wear this." He looked up at Rosé, wincing a bit.

She'd told him to wear it until they entered the 23 Wards. She knew from the very beginning that the count would try shooting him.

"There's no need to show the enemy our hand," she replied, unfazed.

"…The enemy?" Yahiro pursed his lips. He didn't expect her to outright say their sponsor was their *enemy*.

"I'd heard rumors that Count Raimat is incredibly fascinated by the Lazarus. It appears they were true; who would've thought he'd come all the way here just to test you?" She grinned.

That helped him realize her true intentions. She was testing the count, just as he had tested Yahiro. She'd brought him as bait to check whether the count really had as much interest in the Lazarus as she had heard. It was very likely she herself had leaked the intel on the Galerie hiring him as a guide.

Both Yahiro and the count had been dancing in the palm of her hand this whole time.

"The operation begins in thirty minutes. You can change out of that uniform now. We have a new one for you in the carrier to your right."

Rosé spoke innocently, as though none of this had been her plan all along.

"You even had a change of clothes at the ready?" he said wryly.

Rosé was still unfazed, however. She held her hands together and smiled pityingly.

"Oh, but we don't have a change of underwear. Sorry about that."

"I told you I didn't soil myself!" he screamed.

The operators all burst out laughing at that.

It was the first time since he became the Lazarus that he heard the laughter of comrades.

3

There was a girl with green eyes in the mirror.

Her skin was flawless. Silver eye shadow. Lavender lips. Silver hair with a gentle wave tied up in pigtails.

Her new outfit, based on a fairy design, was a bit embarrassing, actually–her shoulders were exposed. The design itself was very delicate and cute, however. She convinced herself everything would be all right so long as she stayed in character and turned to face the camera. It was showtime.

"Waooon! Hi, everywaon, Iroha Waon here!"

She said her usual greeting after unmuting the mic, hoping it would eventually reach her brethren.

✝

"So then, I told them: *'Sorry, only pedestrians and nonmotorized vehicles past this point.'* You should've seen that, man! It was hilarious! Ha-ha-ha!"

"Y-yeah…" Yahiro nodded tiredly.

Josh had been chattering incessantly ever since Operation: Kushinada Hunt began. Now Yahiro knew about the guy's upbringing and history, his likes and dislikes in food and even women, everything.

"Woooo, that's chilly!" Captain Giuli leaned over the broadside, delighting in the spray of the water on her cheeks.

The troops were on two rigid-hulled inflatable boats, sailing the Sumida River.

"I never would've thought of taking the water route! Great idea, Yahiro," Josh said with wonder.

Tokyo had this image of a cluster of high-rise buildings, but in truth, ever since the Edo period, it had been a river city, flourishing thanks to the waterways. Yahiro's master plan to reach their destination safely was just that: avoid land routes as much as possible.

"There are few aquatic Moujuu, and their emergence points are mostly fixed," Yahiro said while opening up the map to check their location.

A group of humans moving together would obviously alert the Moujuu. Taking an entire squad of operators all the way to the city center unharmed was virtually impossible, even for someone as knowledgeable about the 23 Wards as Yahiro. Using the water route was his last resort in trying to overthrow those odds.

"Problem is, we have no escape if we come across one..." He narrowed his eyes and looked forward.

An aquatic Moujuu rose to the surface and approached the boats. Its skin was thick and slimy, its appearance similar to that of a sea slug.

"That's what we're here for!" Josh aimed his special forces light-weight machine gun at it before Yahiro could give any orders, and he immediately opened fire.

The boat rocked violently, but Josh's aim was nothing to scoff at. All bullets hit the target despite the instability and the more than 182 meters of distance.

The other boat, transporting Rosé, provided cover fire at the same time.

Killing a Moujuu with light machine guns was unlikely, but it did have the effect of scaring it away from the boats' path. It flinched and dove back into the water, and they took the chance to pass right through.

Once he was at a safe distance, Josh lowered his gun.

Then a blast not unlike fireworks echoed from afar. It came from a tank's revolver cannon. One of the other PMCs had begun fighting Moujuu on land.

"Whoa... They're going all out," Josh muttered while looking in the direction of the noise.

"Ranga Patna's armored corps... Doesn't sound like they're doing well...," Paola said while equipping a new ammunition belt to her gun.

Amid the gunfire, they could hear the sound of the tanks crashing into buildings and their armor getting crushed. Still, it didn't sound like they were getting completely overwhelmed, but they were suffering some serious losses. And the longer the fight raged on, the more Moujuu would gather, and the greater their disadvantage.

"Hate to say it, but that chairman was right. All the Moujuu are gonna go there, keeping us relatively safer."

"Don't forget...we, too...were supposed to do that for them...," Paola replied to Josh just as serenely.

Exemplary PMC employees—precise judgment even while filled with disgust.

They could divide the Moujuu's attention by having multiple different troops march to the destination. It was the only way to smoothly reach the city's center, even by water.

That didn't mean the other squads were voluntarily playing the bait, however. No, everyone was thinking the same thing: They hoped for the chance to get the upper hand and beat the others to the treasure.

As proof of that, white trails were painted on the sky above. Aircraft trying to cross the 23 Wards by air.

Giuli took notice of that and wailed in pity.

"Oof...so they're doing that."

"Huh?" Yahiro also looked up, narrowing his eyes at the brightness.

His expression quickly darkened. He noticed the puffy objects descending from the aircraft.

"That's a QDS Hercules... Paratrooper transport...," Paola explained while looking through her sniper scope.

QDS was one of the PMCs participating in Operation: Kushinada Hunt—Queensland Defense Service. They had decided to take neither the land nor water route: They were trying to send military parachutists right to the Tokyo Dome ruins.

"Parachuting? Hold on, that's not fair," Josh blurted out.

"Idiots," Yahiro whispered in a low voice. The skies of the 23 Wards at any height below the stratosphere were a no-fly zone. He couldn't believe there was a PMC that didn't know the reason.

From their position downriver, they could see the moment the first operator opened his parachute and when the city skyline wavered. A seemingly infinite number of creatures took to the skies from the ruins all over the city. Flying Moujuu. Spectral birds.

"People in parachutes are just Moujuu bait. I was hoping they wouldn't notice with them opening at low altitudes, but...I guess even then, they're just sitting ducks." Yahiro grimaced.

Moujuu had sharp senses; they always noticed whenever someone intruded on their territory. The flying beasts swarmed the QDS operators.

They had opened their parachutes not even a thousand feet from the ground, but that was still too high an altitude. They were unable to move in the air while the Moujuu attacked.

A red mist fell over everything. A bloody haze.

Yahiro and the rest were fortunate enough to be far away from them. They couldn't hear the screams.

Hundreds of Moujuu darted through the skies as they annihilated the QDS troops before any of the forty could reach the ground.

The Galerie's operators observed in silence. They knew well how fearsome the Moujuu were. The way they quickly took care of the pseudo–sea slug a few moments back was proof they had plenty of experience. However, it wasn't until one actually witnessed the sheer numbers and brutality of the beasts emerging in the quarantine area that one could truly understand what they were up against.

"Shit… The 23 Wards are so messed up, man." Josh sighed.

They are. They really are.

This was what Tokyo, Yahiro's former home, had become.

4

"It was our mission, dude. You get that? The mission! But no, that asshole chief had to go and do that!" Josh's chattering did not stop even as he shot at the Moujuu surfacing from the water.

He was American, of Irish descent, and a former cop. He had worked undercover investigating drug cartels until one day, he got involved with the cartel boss's mistress, so he ended up running away to Galerie Berith. He had a colorful history.

According to Josh, all operators in the Galerie had similar stories. Maybe it was because they were all weirdos and outcasts that they decided to join a troop led by a couple of teenage twins.

Despite the eccentricity, though, they were all undoubtedly skilled.

They had blown past six Moujuu encounters and were already 80 percent done with the boat trip. They just had to enter the Kanda River before Ryogoku Bridge, and the Tokyo Dome would be just ahead.

"Things have been going well only because they've been showing up one by one. It's gonna get tricky if they show up in groups with a leader," Josh muttered after defeating the seventh Moujuu, using up nearly twenty grenade shots.

It was then that Yahiro remembered their objective: capture the Kushinada, a Moujuu leading other Moujuu. That would be tricky for sure.

If left alone, it could become a threat to humanity outside the quarantine area. And if captured, its powers could be used by the military and cause conflict among humans. Either way it went, only bloodshed awaited. What was the right thing to do?

Yahiro was not interested in the Kushinada, however. He was merely a guide. His contract with the twins would end as soon as they reached its nest.

What was important to him wasn't this new kind of Moujuu—it was his sister.

Soon he would get details about her whereabouts. After four years of searching for her. He clenched his teeth, staring at his hands.

"Let me correct you on that. Them being alone doesn't mean we can defeat them." Giuli stood up, her orange hair fluttering with the wind.

"Something wrong, Princess?" Josh furrowed his brow when he saw Giuli leaning over the boat's bow.

She did not respond. She only stared intently at the water in front of her.

Then Yahiro noticed the peculiar yellow color of the bridge. They were near the pier of the Kuramae Bridge. And the color of the water was different. A giant Moujuu was lurking beneath.

"Rosetta, stop the boat! It's Bā Xià!" Yahiro yelled to the vessel behind them.

His voice reached the second boat thanks to the integrated comms on the uniform.

He did not expect the response that followed, however.

"It's Rosé."

"What?"

"I told you to call me Rosé."

"This is not the time!"

Right as Yahiro was replying back in desperation, the water shot up like a geyser.

It was fifteen meters tall. It looked like a Mosasaurus—an extinct, colossal sea reptile with fins for forelimbs. Its torso, however, was protected by a tough shell, just like a turtle's.

It was named Bā Xià based on its appearance, for the Chinese mythological creature. It was as astonishing and ferocious as one would imagine from its name. It was one of the five strongest aquatic Moujuu Yahiro knew of.

"Guns won't work?! Paola, blow it away!" Josh urged her.

"I can't promise anything…" She held up the revolver-type grenade launcher armed with six shots.

She launched all six of the high-explosive dual-purpose shots in a row. They had low initial velocity and accuracy but were powerful enough to destroy armored vehicles. And yet, they barely made the giant ashen Moujuu flinch.

"It's not working?" Paola threw the grenade launcher away and grabbed her light machine gun. There was no hope of 6.5mm rifle bullets making a dent in the monster that resisted those grenades, though.

They could only hope to defeat it with a tank gun, if even that. It wasn't named after a mythological monster for nothing.

"Okay, don't shoot. Guess I'll take care of it. Giuli, ram the boat into it." Yahiro stood up with a sigh and languidly instructed his employer. He took out the big knife from the sheath on his leg.

"You'll…take care of it? With that knife?" Paola was dumbfounded.

"I mean, I wish I didn't have to, but here we are." Yahiro shook his head weakly.

Then he stabbed his own left arm. He buried the blade all the way down, drenching it in crimson. He grimaced in pain.

"Whoa! What're you doing, Yahiro?!"

"This is why I said I wish I didn't have to...do it!"

Josh stared at him, mouth agape, as he forcefully pulled out the knife. The blade was entirely covered in sticky, lustrous blood.

Then Bā Xià roared. Its giant eyes stared at Yahiro's bloody blade. Murderous rage dominated its expression. Rage, hatred, and fear.

"We're going full throttle! Everyone hang on to something!" Giuli grabbed the helm before any of the operators could wrap their heads around what was happening, and she merrily accelerated without hesitation.

"We're doing this?" Josh shrieked.

"You're going down, turtle!" Yahiro leaped off the bow without much run-up.

Parts of the riverbank of the Sumida were collapsing, abandoned boat remains and timber floating all over the Moujuu nest. Yahiro used them as a foothold on his way to Bā Xià. The Moujuu lost track of him, its jaws vainly chomping the air.

Giuli's boat collided with the beast but managed not to capsize. Yahiro stabbed Bā Xià's shoulder with his knife and used it as support to climb on its back.

Starting from the stab wound, Bā Xià's body began to change. Black miasma shot out of it like blood, and its skin—capable of resisting grenade explosions—began to crumble. The damage was limited, however. The affected area on the Moujuu's huge body was too small, comparatively—far from a lethal wound.

"Should've known it wouldn't be that easy against a big guy."

Bā Xià rampaged. Yahiro gripped its back so it couldn't buck him off, then slashed his left arm once more.

Yahiro's blood was poisonous to the Moujuu. He did not want Rosé et al knowing, but defeating Bā Xià without this power was not possible. He wounded the beast's back once again with his bloody blade, then poured the fluid flowing from his wrist into the cut.

"How's that tasty blood for ya, huh?!" Yahiro grinned savagely, all the while getting light-headed from the blood loss.

Moujuu exuded miasma in explosive bursts when they came into contact with his blood. This mist was toxic for regular humans, but he resisted the potent acid-like substance with his jaw clenched.

Bā Xià roared in pain, and the bridge creaked from its rampage.

Its resistance was over soon enough. Its movements became sluggish as Yahiro's poison spread throughout its body, until it finally went completely silent.

"Good job, Yahiro. I'll have them pick you up right away so you can continue guiding us. We lost a fair amount of time with that." Rosé's cool voice echoed into Yahiro's ear as he breathed heavily where he leaned against the monster's back.

Just as she said, Giuli's boat soon approached him. The twins had no intention of letting him rest. Talk about exploitative employers.

"That was amazing... You killed that giant with a knife!" Josh shook his head in disbelief while looking back at the defeated Bā Xià's body.

All the other operators seemed to think the same.

I know, right? he thought without much enthusiasm.

They had their doubts about him really being immortal, but now they knew he was just as much of a monster as the Moujuu were.

Would they ostracize him? Persecute him? It could go either way, honestly. He wouldn't feel bad about it, though. He was already used to the loneliness. In the end, he was but a contractor, and he wasn't looking for anything out of this other than info on his sister.

"Yahiro... You okay?" Paola asked the Lazarus, who was in one corner of the boat.

Yahiro couldn't understand the question for a moment. He followed her gaze and noticed she was talking about his left arm.

"I'm fine. It's recovered already."

He lifted his arm. The uniform was still cut up, but his skin beneath the cloth had already healed, courtesy of the Lazarus blessings.

"What…did you do back there?" She asked a second question.

Yahiro shrugged. He wasn't getting out of this one.

"My blood is poison to the Moujuu. Though I guess I haven't tried it on *all* of them."

"Poison? That was poison? The turtle just crumbled like *bam!*" Josh snapped his fingers; it was the opposite reaction Yahiro was expecting. "I see, so that's how you've been surviving in the 23 Wards. I knew you'd be no ordinary kid, since the Princess brought you and all, but man… Wait, hold on, doesn't that mean we could exterminate the Moujuu with your blood?" Josh said with great excitement.

Yahiro shook his head with an awkward smile. Perhaps he had talked too much, but they would have eventually found out.

"It's not that convenient. The blood rapidly loses its effects after it leaves my body."

It was more like it went out of his control, to be more precise. Blood that completely left his body was no longer his, the Lazarus's. It was no different from any other substance. Shooting bloody arrows from a safe distance didn't work, which was why he used only a knife.

"Whoa, what's with that knife? It's all worn out." Josh's eyes went wide as he saw Yahiro sheathe it.

"Oh, it's just… They turn out like this after being in contact with my blood for an extended period of time."

The nearly new knife was all chipped now, barely maintaining its original appearance. It was rusted red like a thousand-years-old antique.

"It…can't withstand the touch of your blood?" Paola asked with a stern look on her face.

Yahiro smiled self-deprecatingly and nodded.

"Yeah, so you better not get too close to me. No way something that's so poisonous to Moujuu could be safe for humans. They're not wrong when they call me the cursed Japane—"

"Hmm... I wonder, though..." Giuli interrupted Yahiro with a lighthearted tone.

Yahiro stared at her in confusion. The orange-haired girl leaned over to him and stuck out her tongue. He immediately froze up at the soft sensation on his cheek. It took him a second to realize she had licked a drop of his blood.

"Giuli?! Wh-what're you doing?!"

"See? I'm fine. So don't worry." She stuck out her tongue again cutely and smiled mischievously.

"Yahiro doesn't seem fine, though."

"You're red...like a tomato..."

Josh and Paola grinned, teasing him. The other operators clearly were thinking the same thing, though they said nothing.

"I'm... I'm not...!" Yahiro tried to argue back, but he was too flustered to come up with a retort.

"Good to know the Lazarus is no different from any other teenage boy. Don't worry—I'll teach you how to seduce a woman if we make it back alive."

"Just...don't fall for Giuli... You should see the look on Rosé's face right now."

Josh cheerily grabbed his shoulder, while Paola looked away.

Rosé was staring at Yahiro from the boat behind them. No emotions. Not even winking. He didn't need Paola's warning to know she loved her twin sister excessively, and what she would think after seeing her lick a man's face.

"I didn't do anything, though!"

Yahiro looked weakly at the sky, weariness weighing down his body.

What frightened him the most was Rosé's prolonged silence.

5

Count Hector Raimat received the report at the Japanese branch of Raimat International. RMS's young communications officer read the recon drone's findings out loud with a confused expression.

"Galerie Berith's troop defeated Bā Xià near the Kuramae Bridge."

"Bā Xià?" The count's face twisted in suspicion as he leaned forward in the unadorned, spartan chair.

Raimat International was using the former JGSDF Camp Omiya building as its base. Everything, including the communications network and furniture, had already been there. Considering how the chair felt to sit on, he surmised the Japanese Self-Defense Forces hadn't been a very wealthy organization.

"I heard they sent only one squad of operators into the 23 Wards... How could they possibly defeat a large Moujuu, Grade III, without a tank?"

"We don't know the details, but no large-scale bombardments were observed." The officer simply read what was on his tablet.

The count's brow furrowed.

"Grades" were indicators of a Moujuu's threat level, based on existing military powers. Each grade was four times stronger than the last.

Grade-I Moujuu could be taken care of by one infantry squad, and infantry was only of use up to Grade II. Grade III and higher needed tank support.

And yet, Galerie's troops had supposedly defeated Bā Xià, Grade III. Which meant they held some sort of power Raimat didn't know about.

"The Lazarus... Is it true?" the count muttered gravely. The spark in his eyes put the comms officer on edge. "What about Major La Hire's troops?"

"They are currently heading south through National Route 17, near the Hakusan-ue Intersection. They are less than three kilometers from the goal."

"Tell him about what Galerie Berith did. It shouldn't be a problem, but he should be made aware of it."

"Yes, sir! Right away!" The officer saluted like a soldier before running from the room.

The count waited for his subordinate to be out of his sight before standing up.

His displeased expression remained as he headed to a newly built chalk structure within the premises. A securely isolated facility similar to that of a pharmaceutical laboratory.

"How's Brynhildr looking, Sir Nathan?"

The count went through multiple biometric checks before entering the pressurized lab.

Behind the glass window at the end of the room, like a large aquarium, lay the patient. A girl with white hair wearing a thin hospital gown. Multiple tubes were connected to her body, leading to countless pieces of diagnostic equipment. Curiously, the unconscious girl was restrained by heavy silver chains.

Brynhildr was the name of a demigoddess from Norse mythology. A valkyrie who was said to sleep with armor on. They gave her the name due to her importance as a special test subject.

"No big changes so far. The polysomnograph shows her in slow-wave sleep—deep non-REM sleep."

Near the glass wall stood Auguste Nathan. He slowly turned around to face the count. He was a tall Black man wearing a white coat. Not a Raimat employee. Brynhildr was not the count's, either. He was merely lending them the lab; they were partners.

"What about small changes?"

Nathan's report was standard, but he felt something was slightly different from usual, so he reworded the question.

Nathan glanced at the indicator before him.

"Low-frequency brain activity in the occipital cortexes has decreased, and I've been observing a constant increase of high-frequency activity in others. This is happening as we speak, in fact."

"Mind explaining that in English?"

"...She's dreaming," he replied bluntly to the count's annoyed remark.

People usually had dreams when sleeping, and that was no different for this test subject. The confirmation of it, however, was nothing short of surprising. He hadn't thought of her as useful for anything save as a guinea pig up to this point.

"What about the Red Gold?" The count changed the subject, losing interest in the girl's condition.

Nathan looked at him suspiciously.

"I gave the major the improved Mod-2 F-med. We should wait for his report."

"Not that. I mean the real Gold." The count raised his voice.

The F-med would be a fantastic product once completed, but it wasn't what he truly wanted. Nathan knew that, and still, he shook his head emphatically.

"Unfortunately, Count, we still have a long way to go before her awakening, and we need a conscious weapon in order to obtain the Ichor."

"So we have no choice but to capture the Kushinada... Fine. I will see you around, Sir Nathan."

The count turned his back on Nathan, hiding his restlessness and disappointment. He glanced to the slumbering test subject beyond the glass before exiting the room, saying:

"Enjoy your dreams while they last, Deadly Maiden."

The white-haired girl continued to smile faintly as she slept.

†

"Whoa! Why?! I was so close! So close to perfection! Gosh, why do I always mess it up at the very end?!

"Oh, anyway, rhythm games are very fun! Been a long time since I streamed one. Let's do one more! One and we're done. And I'll choose...this one. I love this song! It was everywhere back when I was in grade school... Ah... No, wait, I'm seventeen thousand years old, so... Forget it!

"Wait, sorry, I'm streaming... What? No way! Enemies?!

"........

"'The stream has ended.'"

†

"Yahiro, what is this?" Rosé asked in a monotone, staring at the orderly farm before her eyes.

The lush green leaves swayed in the wind, glittering under the strong summer sunshine.

"Cucumbers. And...those are tomatoes and green soybeans," Yahiro replied absentmindedly as he looked out at the field of crops.

The vibrant and juicy-looking vegetables were nearly ripe for harvesting.

"Wow... This is what Japanese cucumbers look like? They're different from what I'm used to," Giuli muttered with childlike wonder as she crouched beside the furrows.

Her sister and the operators looked on with warm smiles.

"No, wait. That's gotta be wrong! How in the world is there a cucumber plot smack in the middle of the 23 Wards?!" Yahiro objected, being the only rational one remaining.

They had left the inflatable boats back at the Kanda River and were now at the ruins of the Tokyo Dome.

This area had suffered particularly heavy damage from the J-nocide—the buildings surrounding Suidobashi Station were wrecked beyond recognition. The Tokyo Dome itself had also vanished, leaving only a giant crater behind.

They had found the vegetable field at the garden adjacent to the crater: what had once been the Koishikawa Korakuen metropolitan garden.

The place wasn't expansive. Just barely bigger than a homemade veggie garden. It was well maintained, though—tidily plowed and without weeds. An unthinkable sight to be found right in the middle of Moujuu territory.

"Yahiro, what's that flag? What does it mean?" Josh noticed a swaying cloth near the back of the field while he was on the watch for Moujuu.

It was awfully colorful, about three feet wide. A bit faded but still vivid enough for Yahiro to figure out the drawing on it: a character from a children's anime.

"That's no flag; that's a kiddie bedsheet. It's laundry."

"Laundry?" Josh repeated, bewildered.

Yahiro had heard some countries didn't have the habit of drying laundry outdoors. Perhaps he found it strange that someone was doing that here without worrying about how it looked from outside or any safety concerns.

That wasn't the issue here, though. The bedsheet, held tightly by a couple of clothespins, had clearly been put out to dry not long ago. It hadn't been there for four years, at least.

"Ah…!" someone exclaimed from right beside Yahiro.

A steel bucket fell to the ground with a high-pitched clang.

There was a girl wearing a straw hat on the other side of the cucumber patch. A young boy with a baseball cap stood beside her. Both of them looked younger than Yahiro, like just before middle school age.

"Ch-children? How are there human kids in here?" His jaw hit the ground, and he even forgot to grab his knife in caution.

It didn't make any sense. Was he dreaming?

"Wh-who are you?" the straw-hat girl asked, voice cracking, and placed herself in front of the boy.

Yahiro was flabbergasted. She spoke Japanese.

"You're…Japanese?" He took one step toward her out of reflex. The girl froze up in reaction, pure terror in her eyes.

"Noooo! H-help! Mama!"

"Uwaaaah!"

Yahiro, too, froze at their shrieking. He was used to being shunned for being Japanese, but no one had ever been frightened at the sight of him.

The cap-wearing boy grabbed a tomato and threw it at him. It smashed right into his shoulder.

Josh yelled right away. "Yahiro!"

It's just a tomato, man. His calm was short-lived, however. Yahiro felt a tremor, like an earthquake, and then realized why Josh had warned him.

A giant figure had landed right on the other side of the field. A baboon-like creature nearly three meters tall. Its whole body was covered in tiger-striped bristles. Three claws at the end of each arm. Two giant horns on its head. A Moujuu.

"Don't shoot! You'll hit the kids!" Giuli kicked Josh's machine gun right as he was taking aim.

Yahiro jumped back and unsheathed his knife.

But strangely, the Moujuu did not attack. The tiger-striped beast stayed before the children, growling at the squad of operators.

"The Moujuu's…protecting them? Why…?" Yahiro was baffled at the sight.

Japanese survivors were wary of him and getting guarded by a Moujuu. How in the world did this make any sense?

The tiger-striped Moujuu appeared to be between Grade I and II. The Galerie could defeat it without much trouble. But it appeared to be protecting the children without any intent of attacking. He couldn't bring himself to be the first to strike. And the Galerie's operators were hesitating as well.

The Moujuu lost its patience, seeing how they wouldn't run, and roared once again. Yahiro reflexively raised his knife into position.

Then there was a white flash before his eyes.

"—?!"

The ground burst open, the shock blowing him backward.

Electrical currents ran through his whole body. The air stank of ozone. It was as though he had been struck by lightning. It wasn't nature, though—it was an attack meant to push him back.

"Mama…!"

"Iroha!"

The baseball-cap boy's and straw-hat girl's faces lit up in relief.

Then another lightning bolt struck the ground right in front of Yahiro.

A tornado shook the crop field.

A giant Moujuu landed before them with a violent howl.

It looked like a ferocious amalgam of a wolf, a fox, and a tiger. Its body was around six to eight meters long, excluding its long tail. Its beautiful pure-white fur let off blue sparks.

It had to be Grade III or stronger. Judging from its agility and the power of its electric shocks, it was much more dangerous than Bā Xià. Its appearance and powers were reminiscent of the Raiju—a thunder beast from Japanese mythology.

But what amazed Yahiro the most wasn't the Moujuu. It was the figure on its back. A human woman was riding the beast.

Her long hair fluttered in the wind. She wore a fashionable pair of high-top sneakers and a miniskirt. A maroon school jacket on top. She looked to be about Yahiro's age. She was a teenager.

"You two get inside! Rinka, take care of Kyota!" the girl on the Moujuu yelled in Japanese.

The straw-hat girl nodded hurriedly and grabbed the boy's hand before running away.

The pure-white Raiju snarled, and the tiger-striped Moujuu ran after the kids. They were acting like bodyguards—loyal, competent ones.

"H-hey!" Yahiro reached his hand out after them unconsciously.

Then lightning struck at his feet.

The Raiju glared at him with golden eyes. He could tell it had held back its power for that strike, and still, it could have killed him had he taken another step forward.

"Don't move!" the girl in the school jacket yelled at him. "Who are you?! What do you want?!"

"Who are *you*?! Are you even human?!" Yahiro yelled back, gripping his knife tightly.

The girl had full control of the atrocious beasts—perhaps it wasn't the Lazarus's place to judge, but she couldn't possibly be a regular human.

She narrowed her eyes and puffed out her cheeks in a slight pout.

"What? What am I if not human? You thought I was an angel or something?"

"...Well, that's shameless... You say that while wearing a PE jacket?"

Yahiro was more impressed than shocked at how easily she called herself an angel. Though, sure enough, only someone that sure of themselves would ever try riding a Moujuu.

"Sh-shaddup! Who cares?! Put that knife down or I'm gonna make Nuemaru bite you!" She yelled hard, trying to distract from her reddening face.

Josh and the rest observed in silence as they talked; they did not understand the girl's warning, for they did not speak Japanese.

"Nuemaru? You mean that Moujuu? What in the worl–?"

A sudden gunshot interrupted Yahiro. It wasn't a Galerie operator who had shot. It came from behind the girl in the jacket. From the direction in which the kids had run.

"Wait, there's more of you?!" the girl asked him, pale in the face.

"More of us?" Yahiro looked around in confusion.

All Galerie operators deployed into the 23 Wards were there.

It couldn't have been anyone besides the other PMCs participating in Operation: Kushinada Hunt. Which meant there was another troop who had made its way to the Moujuu's nest just as fast as or even faster than the Galerie.

The girl on the Raiju judged it was no use talking any more with Yahiro. She placed her hand on the white beast's neck and prayed:

"Nuemaru!"

The Moujuu let out a brief howl, then turned its back on them without hesitation.

The girl and the beast sparked away as Yahiro and the rest could only stand and watch.

6

"Who...was that woman?" Yahiro returned and approached the twins.

Giuli and Rosé were the only ones who looked unfazed; everyone else was ready to flee at any moment since coming across the Moujuu tamer. The sisters looked amused, even.

"Kushinada. That was the Kushinada," Giuli said while munching on a freshly picked cucumber.

"...What?" Yahiro blinked repeatedly.

Kushinada. The mysterious entity that was leading the Moujuu herd within the 23 Wards. The reason why leading arms manufacturer Raimat International had called on four different PMCs for help.

"We told you from the very beginning the Moujuu had a leader." Rosé sighed like a detective disappointed in her thick assistant.

"And you knew she was Japanese all this time?!"

"We had considered it. We did not imagine she had a family, though." She showed no shame.

Yahiro was bewildered by the word *family*. Then he remembered the kids had called her *mama*.

"Lady, RMS is here. They started fighting Moujuu up north.

What should we do?" Josh asked Rosé after receiving a report from his subordinate.

"Nothing yet. We don't want them taking Kushinada away, but it's not like we could just attack an associate," Rosé responded calmly. She turned on the comms device on the collar of her uniform and said, "Where did the kids run to?"

"*I will send you the location right away,*" Wei answered. It was then that Yahiro noticed he was missing.

He was following them? With everything that was going on? No, did Rosé let them go in order to find where they're hiding?

"Keep your team searching the area. They might have other escape routes. Avoid any encounter with Moujuu."

"*Roger,*" Wei replied before Rosé cut the transmission.

"What're you gonna do with the kids?" Yahiro glared at her.

Rosé answered matter-of-factly. "Secure them. Negotiations with Kushinada would go better that way."

"You're taking them hostage?"

"I suppose you could put it like that," she admitted.

Yahiro was stunned into silence. That girl—they called her Iroha—had control over Moujuu. Perhaps taking hostages was the best way to face her. If he was okay with using little kids for that purpose, that is.

"Or are you gonna kill Nuemaru like you did that turtle?" Giuli asked innocently.

"I..." Yahiro looked away on reflex.

He'd never hesitated to kill a Moujuu before this. Not doing so would have resulted in his own death. There was no room for hesitation when making such a choice.

However, Nuemaru, that white Moujuu, and the tiger-striped one hadn't tried to attack any humans. Was he prepared to kill *them*?

Rosé stared bemusedly at him hesitating and put down the rifle case she was carrying on her back. Inside it was not a gun but something thin and long wrapped in waterproof cloth.

"If Kushinada wants to protect the children, then she will come back. So here, Yahiro."

"What?"

"Your knife's no good anymore, right? Take it."

Yahiro received the wrapped object he was given. It was much heavier than it seemed. He unwrapped the waterproof cloth, and his jaw dropped at the sight of what was inside.

"This is the katana I salvaged!"

"Kuyo Masakane...The legendary sword said to have been forged in Mizuchi blood by Masakane, a mythical swordsmith who supposedly lived for nearly eight hundred years, from the early Heian period to the end of the Sengoku era."

"Eight hundred years... That's gotta be wrong."

"Most likely. But don't you find it to be a perfect fit for you, Mr. Lazarus?" Rosé kept a straight face.

Yahiro pursed his lips. Truth be told, this wouldn't be his first time wielding a real sword. He used knives only because katanas were hard to come by, but he loved their reach and razor-sharp edge. It would most definitely be the perfect weapon to use against large Moujuu like Nuemaru.

"I'm not paying for this."

"Take it as added recompense for your services. I need you to persuade them."

"What? You want me to talk to that woman?" Yahiro frowned.

Their first encounter couldn't have gone worse, but he, as a fellow Japanese, was still the best option to communicate with her. No one else knew their language.

"No, I mean the children. We need to win them over first."

"I'm just a guide, remember?"

"Yes, if you want to go home right now, I won't stop you." She looked him straight in the eye.

It was as though her gaze was asking him if he really could abandon the Japanese survivors.

Yahiro sighed.

He wasn't happy about playing into her hands, but he couldn't just step down. Not solely because they were Japanese—as a guy with blood that was poisonous to Moujuu, he felt something about his encounter with this girl, who could tame them. It was something akin to fate.

"...You just want me to convince them we're not the enemy?"

"Yes. I could let Giuli do it, but I think having another Japanese person do it would be best."

"Giuli?"

I think you would be the eloquent one. Yahiro tilted his head.

Rosé noticed his doubt and closed her eyes.

"I tend to frighten children."

"O-oh."

Rosé seemed bummed out, despite her unchanging expression.

7

The building was about 183 meters away from the cucumber patch, standing proudly at the edge of the crater. It looked like it used to be a public recreational facility. About 70 percent of its original construction had been destroyed in the aftermath of the J-nocide, but the remains were plenty big enough for a few children to live in.

"People are living in here?" Yahiro couldn't hide his bewilderment after meeting with Wei's team.

There was laundry out, as well as ploughs and hoes. There were even soccer balls and other toys. There was no doubt this place was a dwelling.

"Yahiro! Moujuu! Three o'clock!" Josh yelled from behind.

"Not now, dammit!" Yahiro gritted his teeth, brought the sword down from his shoulder and gripped it in his left hand.

The Tokyo Dome surroundings were extremely dangerous, with

a high Moujuu-appearance ratio. There was nothing preventing stray Moujuu from emerging in the Kushinada's territory.

Three new beasts popped up. They were all different kinds but small, around Grade I. They had one of the most common appearances, but they acted strangely. They charged with no rhyme or reason, as though escaping from something.

"*Wait...Josh... Those Moujuu...,*" Paola chimed in through the comms, stopping Josh's team as they held up their machine guns.

Immediately after, a different pair of Moujuu stood before the three strays. Yahiro knew one of them: It was the tiger-striped beast that had protected the children back at the field.

"*The Moujuu...are killing one another...?*"

"They're trying to protect that building?"

Paola and Josh exclaimed nearly simultaneously.

The tiger-striped Moujuu had attacked the other three beasts before they could get near the building. Seeing Moujuu fight with one another wasn't that rare, but this situation certainly was. One side was trying to protect human children. They were coexisting with humans.

"Is this the power of the Kushinada?" Chills ran down Yahiro's spine.

It wasn't until he saw it in action that he understood how dangerous Kushinada could be. In the wrong hands, her power over the Moujuu could easily upend military balance in the world.

Her existence, however, was also a spark of hope. With her power, humanity could coexist with the Moujuu, and rebuilding the country ravaged by them would not be impossible.

The stray Moujuu were already losing, severely wounded. Any normal animal would have accepted defeat and run away at that point, but for whatever reason, the panicked beasts did not stop resisting.

In consequence, the tiger-striped beast and its companion were caught by surprise. One of the children didn't run away soon enough: a quiet-looking girl wearing a summer middle school sailor uniform. The strays noticed her.

One of the beasts realized she was their weakness and attacked. A rodent-like Grade-I Moujuu. The black squirrel with thorns all over its body jumped at the girl.

"Eek?!" The girl's face contorted in fear.

The Moujuu's eyes glittered at the sight of its powerless prey.

Then a barrage of lead balls pierced its face from the side. Rosé had emptied the thirty-bullet magazine of her anti-Moujuu PDW on it without regard for the ninety-one-meter distance between them.

The jet-black Moujuu stumbled but landed without trouble. The PDW was far more powerful than a handgun, but it did not deal lethal damage to Moujuu.

Still, it gave them a few seconds. Enough time for Yahiro to approach the beast.

"Get down!" he shouted at the girl as he unsheathed his katana.

Kuyo Masakane had a long and steeply curved body—not an easy weapon to handle, and yet, strangely, it felt right in his hands.

Yahiro slashed his hand to cover the blade in blood, then charged against the Moujuu.

Its effect was dramatic. Black miasma spread all around as the Moujuu collapsed in seconds.

"You okay? Not hurt or anything?" Yahiro glanced at the girl, katana still held downward.

The girl was taken aback by the stranger's question but nodded in response. Asking her in Japanese had been the right choice—she now seemed to believe he was on her side.

The remainder of the battle had drawn to a close.

The two strays were fatally injured and vanished soon enough. The tiger-striped Moujuu glanced at him with caution but didn't show any sign of attacking him, perhaps due to his proximity to the girl in the sailor uniform.

Seems like they'll hear me out now. Yahiro sighed in relief.

Right then, thunder struck before his eyes.

"Ayaho!"

The sparking Moujuu ran at them, rubble flying in its wake. On its back was the girl in the school jacket, Iroha.

The Moujuu stopped amid a cloud of dust, right before them, and Iroha jumped from the back of the beast, not even caring about her skirt flipping up on her way down.

"Get away from her, you...shady man!"

Her hair swayed violently as she stepped between them. Yahiro was a little overwhelmed by her scowl.

"Who're you calling *shady*?!"

"You think a non-shady man would approach a girl with a katana in hand?!" Iroha yelled while spreading her arms to protect the girl behind her.

Yahiro couldn't say anything to that. His senses were out of balance due to the J-nocide, but when you looked at it like that, she was right.

"No, Iroha! He saved me from a stray Moujuu!" the girl in the sailor uniform explained in his stead.

Iroha looked at the girl, surprised, then back at him.

"...He helped you? This weirdo? Are you sure?"

"I'm not a weirdo, PE Jacket Girl!"

"Shut it! It's not like I have much choice in wardro—" she argued back, red in the face, aware of how uncool her clothing was, but then she shut her mouth. She opened her eyes wide instead. "Wait... how do you know this is a PE jacket? Are you...Japanese?"

"Yeah." Yahiro nodded, dumbstruck that it had taken her that long to realize.

Iroha's eyes shone bright with surprise and joy, and she drew nearer to him.

"Really?! Where were you all this time?! Are there any more Japanese survivors?!"

"...There might be some out there, but I don't know any personally."

Yahiro shook his head bluntly, feeling strange after her reaction. "Now, about you. What's up with you? Have you been living here ever since the J-nocide? Why do the Moujuu protect you?"

Iroha looked concerned by the sudden interrogation. Perhaps she didn't know whether to tell the truth about her powers.

"Um... I, uh–" She opened her mouth, determined after a few moments of hesitation, but then a roaring sound cut her off.

The ground shook heavily, as though struck by a giant rock. The building's walls were demolished, and the following blast threw Yahiro and everyone else to the ground.

Two Moujuu vanished in a rain of black miasma and meat lumps.

The tiger-striped Moujuu and its companion died protecting Iroha from the incoming tank shell.

8

"Tabby! Calico!" Iroha screamed in anguish amid the deafening noise of the explosion.

Those must've been the names of those two Moujuu. Yahiro felt like he understood their relationship just by knowing she had names for each of them. They were her family.

"Yahiro, that's an RMS wheeled tank." Wei and his operators ran up to them. He spoke in broken Japanese to avoid frightening Iroha and the girl.

He could see the tank at the top of the gentle hill. It was eight hundred meters away, but there was nothing obstructing the view thanks to the damage from the J-nocide. No human in the area had any hope of surviving if they shot a second time.

The fearsome tank, however, did not shoot at them. Instead, operators approached from three directions. A total of fifty people. Four times Galerie Berith's numbers.

"Why?! Why do you do this?!" Iroha questioned Yahiro, big tears in her eyes.

"Calm down! They aren't with us!" he answered sharply.

They were technically with Galerie Berith in this joint operation, but Yahiro did not consider them allies. He hadn't forgotten about them shooting him three times upon first meeting.

"And you gotta know that Moujuu are enemies to normal humans. They didn't attack you; they were trying to protect you!"

"Who asked for your protection?!" Her voice trembled.

Yahiro knew he wasn't telling the truth, but at least Iroha understood the reality that they were abnormal for coexisting with Moujuu. She couldn't argue anymore.

"Big Sis Mama!"

"Iroha! Ayaho!"

The children inside the destroyed building came running at them. There were six of them, including the two they'd seen at the plantation. All of them grade-school age.

"Ren! Kiri! Honoka, Runa! Are you all okay?! Is anyone hurt?!"

Iroha hugged all of them at once. They were terrified, but they had absolute trust in her. She maintained a brave face to put them at ease.

"Nuemaru, please!"

The white Raiju nodded at Iroha's call and stepped in front of them, then let out a magnificent roar.

Moujuu appeared from all over the ruins in response. Eight of them, each a different kind. They all attacked RMS's troops at once.

The beasts, charmed by the Kushinada's powers, acted to protect her. It was thanks to them that they had survived up to this point right in the middle of the 23 Wards.

"I see... Rosy was right. You're amazing, Kushinada." Giuli was standing beside Yahiro before he realized and spoke to Iroha in Japanese with a sparkle in her eyes.

Iroha narrowed her gaze in confusion, but she judged her as not an enemy, for she was wearing the same uniform as Yahiro.

"Kushinada...? You mean me?"

"Sorry, we didn't know your name, so we called you that. Should we call you Mama instead?"

"I am not your mama," she refused, obviously. They were the same age; who would like a girl your age treating you like a mother?

Giuli dropped her shoulders in disappointment.

"Oh... Okay... Anyway, you should tell them to actually kill the enemy, if you can really control them. You won't intimidate them into running away."

"Kill...? I can't do that..."

"They're going to kill you instead, then." Giuli smiled sadly at her.

Then something happened within the RMS troops. Gunshots had ceased all of a sudden. The operators dropped their guns and faced the Moujuu with their bare fists.

No human could ever stand against a Moujuu's physical prowess. The operators were blown away immediately. They did not die, for the beasts were holding back, but they were far from unharmed; they were alive but just barely.

Still, the operators did not stop fighting. They stood back up like zombies drenched in blood and opposed the Moujuu incessantly.

Soon they underwent changes in appearance. Their physiques were warped, their muscles enlarged. Scales covered their whole bodies, thorns rising from their skin. They were no longer human. They were reptiles on two legs. Lizardmen.

"That's...the same as back then...!" Yahiro grunted.

Their new forms were similar to that of the mysterious operator he had fought with the sisters three days back.

The difference was that the level of monstrosity of these operators was to a markedly higher degree than that man's. They retained nearly no human characteristic, and their strength seemed proportionate to that change.

Iroha's Moujuu could not resist the lizardmen's attack.

Once the first was defeated and the balance broken, the rest happened in the blink of an eye. The lizardmen were more numerous and absolutely disregarded defense; the Moujuu fell one after the other.

Iroha's face paled as she watched this unfold.

Giuli was right. They all died because she'd told Nuemaru to call them and because she'd asked them not to kill any human. The reality of it overwhelmed her.

All eight Moujuu defeated, there was nothing left to stop RMS's invasion.

The lizardmen walked triumphantly toward them. The tank that had attacked first led the group. On it was their commander, Firman La Hire.

"Fafnir soldiers... I see. I wondered how they were able to reach the city's center so quickly. So Raimat has completed the Mod-2," Rosé muttered.

Fafnir soldiers was the official name for the lizardmen. Fafnir was a dragon from Norse mythology, but he was not born one—he was originally a human. He obtained cursed gold and threw away his humanity in order to protect it. The perfect name indeed for RMS's operators who turned into monsters for money.

"I am Firman La Hire. Good job capturing the Kushinada, Galerie Berith." Firman spoke to Rosé from atop the halted tank.

All of Galerie's operators were surrounding Iroha and the kids. It wouldn't be irrational to think they were protecting her.

"RMS will handle her escort. Relinquish her, please." Firman's tone was polite but unwavering.

The Fafnir soldiers lined up and closed in on them little by little. Before they knew it, they were close enough to attack with their superhuman powers at any moment.

"What is the meaning of this, Major Firman? We have the right to keep the Kushinada, as we secured her first, don't we?" Rosé asked serenely.

RMS was a subsidiary of the sponsor of this operation, Raimat International, but they were still only one of the participating companies and on equal standing with the Galerie as far as the contract said.

Firman did not argue against it. He nodded in agreement, then smiled cruelly.

"It's true. But if you happened to disappear, then we would get the right to keep her."

"Josh!"

"Right away!" He shot at the same time Firman swung his arm downward.

Grenades rained down mercilessly over the RMS troops, blowing the Fafnir soldiers away.

Wei and Paola's team joined the attack immediately. They used their machine guns to mow down the RMS operators who had escaped the blast.

The anti-Moujuu bullets did not defeat the Fafnir soldiers, however. They were using an improved version of the drug, Mod-2. Their bodies' endurance and healing capabilities far exceeded the other man Yahiro had fought.

"Tsk...!" Yahiro judged that the Galerie had no hopes of winning and ran toward Firman. He kicked away all human operators guarding him on the way, then thrust his katana up to Firman's throat. "Don't move, Firman La Hire," he warned him.

Firman looked thrilled. Yahiro knew about his quick draw speed, but he didn't seem intent on reaching for his gun.

"What are you trying to do, Japanese boy?"

"Withdraw your troops. You're too old for her, man. Let her go." He knowingly tried to rile him up. He guessed having him lose his cool would make it easier to negotiate.

And yet, Firman kept a straight face, only his eyes turning darker with contempt.

"I thought you were just Galerie Berith's guide."

"I already did my job for that. Though I'm still waiting on the payment."

"I see... So I wouldn't have to pay for damages if I killed you, then." He chuckled.

Firman's hands were held at his shoulders' height in a show of nonresistance, but then a shock ran through Yahiro's torso. A sharp, lancelike object had pierced his abdomen all the way through and out his back.

"What...what did you...?!" Yahiro groaned, spitting blood.

It was a tail. A scaly, steel-blue tail that had pierced his torso. The large limb had come from Firman's backside.

"Fafnir medicine's Mod-3. You're out of luck, kid. I am a perfect dragonman."

Firman cackled as his body took on the appearance of a Fafnir soldier.

What he meant by *perfect dragonman* was that he could change into this form of his own free will, without taking the med. His transformation was complete by the time Yahiro understood this. The strong scales on his neck easily repelled Kuyo Masakane's blade.

"Gh...oh..." Yahiro staggered backward as Firman removed his tail from the boy's torso.

The dragonman raised the claws of his right hand as he watched his opponent with satisfaction.

"Oh, I haven't forgotten about your body armor under that uniform. I will make sure you're really dead this time."

"—?! No! Let him go!" Iroha yelled upon hearing that.

The draconized RMS commander swung his right hand, slashing Yahiro's throat. The boy fell on his back as red blood gushed out, soaking his whole body.

"Noooo!" Iroha wailed, hugging her head.

Yahiro saw her from the corner of his blurry vision and found it strange. She had only just met him; why cry for him? Then he remembered. This was what would've been a normal reaction to death before the J-nocide. She wasn't wrong. It was this world that was wrong.

The white Raiju howled in reaction to Iroha's overflowing emotions. Thunder, stronger than ever, struck all around it, instantly turning a dozen Fafnir soldiers to ash. Lightning continued to strike, detonating the tank by igniting its cannon.

"So this is the power of the Kushinada...," Firman muttered; he sounded impressed but tranquil. "I have nothing to fear now."

Firman dissolved the draconization and drew his gun to shoot at the Raiju.

The bullets had no effect on the Moujuu, naturally. It merely shook its head in irritation after receiving a couple of shots to the face. It seemed suicidal to turn back into a regular human in the face of the raging beast. But did the Raiju notice it was merely provocation to get it away from Iroha?

"Nuemaru?!"

The white Moujuu charged at Firman, but then its upper body was blown away. A boom thundered with a moment's delay. The shot came from a tank waiting eight hundred meters away, its supersonic blast hitting the Raiju with laser accuracy.

Even this strong Moujuu could not resist a tank's shot. The remaining 30 percent of its body fell to the ground and turned to miasma right away.

"No! Nuemaru, this can't be! Nuemaru!!!" Iroha wailed, clinging to the Raiju's remains.

The Fafnir soldiers took advantage of this opening. Even with the power to control Moujuu, Iroha herself was just a helpless girl. She was easily taken away from the Raiju and escorted to Firman.

"It's over, Princess! Lady! We can't keep going anymore!"

"We don't have...enough bullets..."

Josh and Paola shouted as their operators protected Iroha's kids, as the twins had instructed. The situation was beyond their powers now that they had lost the Raiju. The enemy was unarmed, but it took more bullets to fell one Fafnir soldier than a regular human. Ammo was running low.

"We'll be fine. Get ready!" Giuli exclaimed with confidence.

Then the world turned dark. A thunder-like buzz shook the air.

Wyverns, gryphons, insects, any and all flying Moujuu gathered, blanketing the skies. Beasts from all over the 23 Wards reacted to Iroha's wailing.

"We're retreating, Giuli!"

"Got it. Ninja!" Giuli scattered silver cans all around at Rosé's signal, and they expelled the stench of tear gas.

The gas had a stronger effect on the Fafnir soldiers' enhanced senses. They panicked as they were robbed of their vision, and the Galerie's operators began their escape.

"This is ridiculous... She gathered all these Moujuu here?! How?!" Firman was clearly disturbed.

And they weren't only flying Moujuu. Earthbound beasts came out of the ruins and ran toward them. They were not under the complete control of Iroha like the Raiju had been—it was obvious they were merely acting on instinct. One could guess Iroha's powers had run rampant, and she was summoning Moujuu without restraint.

Not even the Fafnir soldiers could possibly stand against this many beasts.

Firman immediately decided to forsake his troops. He had the confidence that he, and only he, could escape the Moujuu's blockade. The question was, should he risk persecution by taking the Kushinada with him?

Firman glanced at Iroha in order to make the decision, but he was shocked at what he found there. The Fafnir soldiers who had captured her were already on the ground, drenched in blood.

Someone else had Iroha in his arms. The supposedly dead Japanese boy. Yahiro. The wounds from Firman's attacks had closed—both his abdomen and throat had healed completely. The only remaining trace of his wounds was the blood soaking his entire body.

"Impossible...!"

Firman shot his gun, drawing it almost unconsciously, but Yahiro stopped the bullet shot from barely a few feet away with his left arm. It didn't pierce his flesh; it bounced off with a spark. His arm was covered in crimson armor.

"No... That arm... Why do you have the Sigurd's power?!"

Firman threw his gun away and raised the claws on his draconized right hand.

"What? I don't know what you're talking about!"

Yahiro's katana moved in a flash. The high-pitched ring of metal clashing echoed throughout. Yahiro's sword had already been repelled by Firman's draconized body once before, but this time, his silver arm broke with a splattering of fresh blood.

"Gaaah!" Firman roared like a monster.

Yahiro turned and ran. The Moujuu herd was attacking everyone indiscriminately. The Galerie's operators were already retreating with the kids. There was no reason to stay there.

"We're out of here, Iroha!" he told the girl as he lifted her up against his side.

"No, don't! I can't leave Nuemaru behind! Go on without me!" Iroha wailed like a child, aggressively shaking her head.

She reached for the Raiju's remains on the ground. Yahiro held her tight so she couldn't wiggle free and ran as fast as he could.

"Noooo!"

The Kushinada's screaming echoed incessantly under the Moujuu-infested sky.

1

Yahiro stopped after almost an hour of running with Iroha under his arm.

He was near the border between the former Bunkyo and Toshima Wards. Right before the old cemetery where the grave of a famous author was located.

Yahiro's pro-athlete–like stamina came from his regenerative ability as the Lazarus. He forced his body to ignore damage to his muscle fibers and the accumulation of acids causing fatigue.

That did not mean fatigue or pain would vanish altogether, however; in fact, his exhaustion only accelerated with the passage of time. That, along with the damage he had already sustained in battle, pushed his body to its limits.

"I think we should be okay now..."

Yahiro entered a random abandoned building before his body stopped moving entirely.

The convenience store inside was in relatively good shape.

Perishables were in a terrible state, but there were a few snacks and canned foods that seemed edible.

It sounded like RMS was still fighting the Moujuu; Yahiro could hear intermittent gunshots from where they had come. They didn't stumble across any beasts, which was why they'd managed to lose RMS in the first place.

"...Damn, that hurts. I'm carrying you for your own good, y'know... You shouldn't be biting and scratching me." Yahiro threw Iroha on the floor while trying to regain his breath.

His arms were numb from exhaustion, but the scratch and bite marks remained in abundance. She'd fought to get him to leave her behind.

"Shaddup. Don't cry from a few scratches..."

Iroha glared at him, eyes swollen red. The sulky look on her face made her appear much younger than when he'd first met her.

"Oh, right, your wounds! Aren't you hurt?! That blondie slashed your neck back there...?" Iroha stood up and asked him in a panic; she had witnessed the moment Firman La Hire killed him.

"Don't worry. I don't die." Yahiro realized it would be no use trying to feign ignorance, and he showed her his neck.

Iroha's eyes opened wide. "What do you mean...you don't die?"

"I'm not really sure. Maybe it's because I'm already dead. I died four years ago..."

Yahiro's blunt tone stunned her to silence.

The J-nocide had happened four years ago; there was no need for further explanation for someone who had lived through that. Surviving the J-nocide was impossible without some sort of miracle or mysterious power. Iroha knew that, for she, too, had such power.

"...Why did you save me?" she asked serenely.

Yahiro ran a hand through his hair and sat down on the floor.

"Dammit... That's what I wanna know..."

"What?! You regret it?! I didn't even ask you to!" She was not expecting that reaction; confusion and anger boiled within her.

"I don't regret it! Not like I had the time to be choosing who to help."
He sighed. "I just didn't want my clients to die. I haven't been paid."

"Clients? What do you mean?" Her voice grew colder.

Yahiro's tone turned careless as well. "I'm a salvager. I fetch art
pieces left behind in the 23 Wards to sell to rich foreigners."

"…That's stealing."

"Maybe. But they'd only deteriorate if left here in Japan, so
maybe it's better for them to be on display in a collector's mansion
overseas, right?"

"Well…that makes sense…" Iroha had trouble responding to
Yahiro's confession to his crimes. "…Wait. If that's your job, then
why'd you even come to us?"

"I told you, I have a client. They asked me to guide them here
to fetch *you*."

"Me…? Why? Is it because I'm pretty?" She blinked in surprise.

"I've been wondering this since we first met. What's up with your
incredibly high self-esteem?" He was dumbfounded.

Sure enough, Iroha had quite the pretty face, though he had a
hard time admitting that right then due to the lousy PE jacket and
her eyes all scrunched up with tears. He could admit her frequent
changes in expression were adorable, though. It was kind of like
watching a pet.

"What I was told, actually, was that they wanted to capture the
boss of the Moujuu. I had no idea it was a woman, much less a
Japanese woman."

"The Moujuu…boss? That doesn't sound right. Nuemaru and
the others are like my family…" Iroha looked downcast, all spirit
from a moment before gone.

Then she slapped herself to try and rouse herself.

"Wait a second. So you heard *the Moujuu's boss* and pictured, like,
an alpha monkey or something?"

"I think my clients had an idea of what you were, though. They
were calling you Kushinada, and now I see why."

"So you were."

He ignored her.

Iroha understood it all then, though. She nodded.

"Right, Kushinada is a Japanese goddess. Goddess, huh… Yeah, they're not wrong."

"Oh my God, shut up…"

"So what were they gonna give you if you captured me?" she asked with irritation in her voice.

Yahiro replied bluntly, "Intel on my sister."

"Huh?"

"My little sister disappeared four years ago, and they're gonna tell me where she is."

"Um… I see. I'm sorry…" Iroha adverted her eyes. She seemed guilty about making him talk about it.

"You don't have to be sorry." Yahiro shrugged with an awkward smile. "Besides, it's not like my clients are dead. They ran away before us, with your kids."

"…Um, excuse me? My kids? What do you mean by that, exactly? You should be saying siblings!" Iroha raised her brows in resistance.

Yahiro looked at her with suspicion. "Siblings? They called you Mama, though?"

"Mamana!"

"What?"

"That's my name! Iroha Mamana!" She pointed at herself.

It took Yahiro a few seconds to understand.

"Ahhh… Okay. That's confusing."

"Shaddup. It's my name! Don't call it *confusing*! That's rude!" She pouted. It didn't look like it was the first time someone had made fun of her name. "And you are?"

"I am?"

"What's your name?! What am I supposed to call you?"

"Yahiro. I'm Yahiro Narusawa."

"Okay, Yahiro. Got it." She nodded. "What's your age?"

"Age? Um, what year is it, again? Well, I was thirteen when the J-nocide started, so…"

"You're seventeen? No way—we're the same age! When's your birthday?"

"Oh, wow…" Yahiro chuckled; it had been a long time since he talked to someone like they were classmates.

"That's so cool, getting to know someone my age again… You know, the kids haven't had an older boy to play with before. I'm sure Ren, Kiri, and Kyota will be so excited to hang out with you…" Iroha smiled as she said their names but spoke between sobs as she kept going. "Oh, but don't you dare try to lay a hand on my sisters. They're such good girls… Ayaho…Rinka…they all are… They're so…" She couldn't keep it in any longer, and her face fell.

They didn't know if the kids were safe after RMS's attack. Her Moujuu had already been killed; there was no one left to protect them.

Yahiro couldn't come up with a way to comfort her. He knew anything he told her would ring hollow.

Even the Galerie would have trouble escaping alive from the chaotic Moujuu-versus-Fafnir-soldier battle. The odds of the small kids surviving that sounded hopeless. And their fate likely wouldn't change even if they had Yahiro and Iroha with them.

She understood that, so she didn't blame Yahiro, and merely continued crying in silence.

Just as he was starting to feel it would be easier for him to take the blame, an electronic beeping broke the silence. Something was vibrating in Yahiro's thigh bag.

"What's…that sound?" Iroha lifted her head, tears still streaming.

"Oh, the thing Giuli gave me…" Yahiro narrowed his eyes as he took out the vibrating bundle from his bag. The chocolate-bar-sized box in the wrapper of a luxury confectionery.

* * *

"Heeey, Yahirooo... Can you see meee?" The girl with orange highlights waved her hand merrily on the screen.

The box was in fact a smartphone-size comms device. The image wasn't smooth, but the sound was clear, with little noise. Reaction time was a bit lagged, perhaps due to complex encryption on the transmission.

"...Giuli? What's this device? You said it was candy," Yahiro started while showing her the torn paper wrapper.

He could have called them much earlier had he known what it was from the beginning; he implied this with annoyance in his voice. Giuli only tilted her head in confusion, though.

"Huh? There was no candy? I put one ramune in there."

"The gadget's an extra?!"

Yahiro noticed one ramune candy at the bottom of the box, and his shoulders sagged. This device was too big to be treated like a bonus toy and way more important than the supposedly main item.

"You've got Kushinada there with you, I see." Rosé changed places with her; she knew the conversation would go nowhere with the elder sister at the helm.

It was then that Yahiro noticed Iroha was also inside the frame of the camera.

"What about you? Did you get out of the 23 Wards? How?"

"I had many options in place for an escape plan. Had to use one of the aces up my sleeve," she replied emotionlessly; she did not seem the least intent on explaining what the plan consisted of.

"No one died?"

"We have a few wounded, but the Galerie's without losses. The Kushinada's... Iroha Mamana's children are also safe."

"Really?! Ayaho's okay?! Everyone's alive?!" Iroha screamed, cutting into the conversation.

Rosé moved the camera around to show the children in the same room. They appeared to be inside a big vehicle. Bench seats on one side had the seven children sitting all together. They seemed fatigued and nervous, but no one was gravely harmed.

"Mama...?"
"Is that Iroha?!"
"Hey, Iroha."

They called her name one after the other.

"Runa... Honoka... I'm so glad..." She fell to her knees in relief and started crying loudly right away.

Which one's the child, I wonder? Yahiro observed in silence. The children also smiled awkwardly.

"So what's with this device?" Yahiro asked Rosé, back on-screen again.

"Encrypted comms. We use this to disguise your location and our conversation."

"So you were expecting Raimat to turn on us from the very beginning." He glared at her.

There was no need for encrypted comms when going against Moujuu. They'd known this would happen all along, and they never told him.

"Hedging risk is basic business practice," Rosé answered composedly. *"But we can only use it one time. By the second, they'd have broken the encryption, and they'd get your precise location. Which is also why we can't talk for long."*

"So we can't let them know my location?" Yahiro asked a question he already knew the answer to.

Rosé nodded.

"Raimat is after you. RMS sent thirty-six more operators to the 23 Wards. And it's likely they're all..."

"Fafnir soldiers, huh?"

"Yes."

Yahiro's expression darkened as he heard her confirm that.

His past two encounters with Fafnir soldiers were enough for him to understand the threat they represented. Their strength and endurance were superhuman. Individually, they were weaker than a Moujuu, but they also had human weaponry and group tactics at their disposal. Yahiro didn't have the confidence he'd be able to escape them again.

"So what should we do?"

"Destroy RMS." Rosé answered Yahiro's serious question like it was nothing. As though she was certain Yahiro could destroy them.

Yahiro couldn't believe how casually she said such a thing.

"Don't be ridiculous! I can't do that alone!"

"I believe you have the right to self-defense under Japanese law."

"That's not the issue! I'm telling you it's impossible! Physically!"

"Then get out of the 23 Wards. But southward, toward Kanagawa. Yes, you could take the Dai-Ichi Keihin highway and cross the Tama River." Rosé gave an alternative plan right away, already expecting Yahiro's refusal of the first.

"Toward Kanagawa...? Are you being serious right now? No salvager has ever entered that area." Yahiro disapproved of the blue-haired girl's new plan for many reasons.

Yahiro and Iroha were at Minami-Ikebukuro. To head to

Kanagawa, they would have to go through the remains of either Shibuya or Minato.

"I know that. They say the area spanning Shibuya and Minato is especially dangerous even inside the 23 Wards. Like it's Moujuu headquarters or something."

"Then why are you—?"

Rosé interrupted his objection. *"Which is why it makes sense to take that route. Did you forget who you have there with you?"*

Yahiro turned to look at Iroha.

"Kushinada…"

The girl who could control Moujuu. If her powers worked even on Moujuu she'd just met, then going to that unexplored zone would be much less dangerous. Quite the opposite, in fact, since they could block RMS's pursuit.

"Anyway, you have no other choice. RMS's reinforcements are coming from Saitama, heading south. Raimat's head-quarters are in the prefecture's capital."

"And once you get to Yokohama, there'll be a ship waiting for you," Giuli stepped in cheerily.

"A ship?" Yahiro furrowed his brow.

Watercraft were an important means of transport in Japan after highways were torn during the J-nocide, but they were slow—unfit for escape. He couldn't imagine things would turn in their favor just because they reached Yokohama.

Rosé cleared Yahiro's doubts: *"We got a Galerie ship on standby at the Yokohama Port. We can get Iroha Mamana out of the country if you reach there. Along with her children, of course."*

"We'll be waiting for you over there!"

"Oh... Hey...!" The transmission was cut off before he could stop them.

Yahiro held the device in hand and frowned as he looked at Iroha.

2

"Those are your clients? Aren't they too young?" Iroha managed to contain her tears as she looked at him with suspicion.

Yahiro wasn't offended by the question. In fact, he agreed.

"I know, right? Well, I suppose they have their reasons."

"I guess... Such cute girls wouldn't be coming to Japan otherwise." She was satisfied with the answer.

Her point of view was a breath of fresh air to him. Perhaps the twins had had a much harder life than he first imagined, born into an arms-dealing family and all.

"Anyway, we've gotta decide what to do now," Yahiro muttered.

Iroha was taken by surprise. "We're not going to Yokohama?"

"Can we really believe what they say?"

"What? Aren't they *your* clients?" she retorted, baffled.

Yahiro frowned. "I just met them three days ago, and this is my first time working for them. I'm not sure how much we can trust them."

"Hmm... I'm sure they're plotting something, but I think they're nice girls." She was oddly full of confidence.

Yahiro opened his eyes wide. "Why?"

"Well, they helped the kids." She puffed out her chest, grinning for whatever reason.

"Maybe they only did that so you would do as they say. The kids might be hostages."

"If a hostage situation was their goal, then there's no reason to save all seven of them. Taking all of them must've been pretty hard when it could've cost them their own lives," she countered.

Yahiro was surprised by how calmly she pointed that out.

Surely the Galerie didn't save them just because they were good people. They must have deemed it necessary in order to get on Iroha's good side. Seen from another angle, this would mean that they valued her just that much. Which would mean that Galerie Berith was trustworthy, at least up until handing Iroha over.

"Why were you raising those kids over there, by the way?" he asked her.

Iroha had called them her *siblings*, but they couldn't possibly be blood related. What, exactly, tied them together? Why was she caring for them? Why smack-dab in the middle of the 23 Wards? He tried getting answers for all of this with one question.

He was taken aback by her answer.

"It wasn't just me taking care of them. We had more people at first. A nurse, an old man good with machines…"

"What happened to them?"

"They all died. It wasn't a Moujuu attack or anything; I think they just couldn't handle the changes in the world. They tried going outside the 23 Wards and got killed by humans," Iroha said flatly, suppressing her emotions.

Yahiro's expression didn't change, and he stayed silent.

Four years had already gone by since the J-nocide. Not a short amount of time during which one had to face drastic changes in the world. It was no surprise that the adults wouldn't be able to cope with the deaths of everyone they knew and the despair of having to live cooped up inside Moujuu territory.

"I see. So that's why the kids were so scared of seeing us."

The pair they had found at the plantation were incredibly wary of them. Humans from outside the 23 Wards had killed the adults close to them—no one from the outside could be seen as an ally. They were all threats.

"I mean, I didn't think we could live inside the 23 Wards forever. I knew the J-nocide was over, and our food is starting to expire."

Even with the vegetable garden, they had too few hands to produce enough food. Their only choice was to rely on preserved foods left over in the businesses of the 23 Wards. Four years had already gone by, and this resource was reaching its limit. They would have no choice but to go outside eventually.

"But I couldn't take Nuemaru or anyone else outside..." Iroha hugged her knees.

Moujuu living in the 23 Wards were seen as a threat, but they were the children's guardians, protecting them from the humans on the outside.

Iroha would have to leave them behind if they tried to go outside, but she wouldn't be able to protect the kids by herself. She had no choice but to remain inside the 23 Wards.

Thus, her weird little community was born.

"I don't think you were wrong," Yahiro said. He meant it. It wasn't about cheering her up more than him expressing his honest praise and envy.

"Huh?"

"The outside is still a living hell. There's just relatively fewer Moujuu."

Iroha bit her lip. She realized that, while she was living together with her siblings, Yahiro was out there all alone.

"What about you? Do you have any siblings or other people who supported you throughout all this?"

"I..." Now *he* was biting *his* lip.

It wasn't as though he had no one to support him emotionally, but he didn't feel comfortable saying it. He'd never minded it before, but trying to put it into words at this moment, it felt quite embarrassing.

"Oh, and now that I think about it, you must not have gotten to speak Japanese much lately, have you? And yet you sound perfectly fluent still. Wouldn't you forget after four years without speaking it?"

"I...think it might be because of this live stream." He opened up to her. If she wanted to laugh about it, then so be it.

"Live stream? On the internet?" Iroha's expression stiffened.

Yahiro nodded. "There's this streamer called Iroha Waon, and she streams in Japanese. She just talks about whatever or cooks on-stream and stuff."

"U-uh-huh..."

"I'm not saying she is my emotional support, but her streams were like a ray of hope. They made me feel like I'm not alone... But anyway, why am I even talking about this?"

"I—I see... Woo, I'm glad, y'know?" She put on an awkward smile and scratched her head.

Yahiro stared, confused, at her; that was a weird reaction.

"What do you mean you're *glad*?"

"Huh? Wait, hold on. You haven't noticed?!" She opened her eyes wide as she drew her face nearer to his. "It's me! I am Iroha Waon! Waooon!"

"C'mon, stop that. It's not funny," Yahiro grumbled.

He was prepared for getting laughed at for the idea of a streamer being his *ray of hope*, but not this. This he couldn't take.

It was Iroha who yelled at him, however.

"What the heck?! You don't believe me?! Here! Look, it's that outfit! Rinka sewed it for me!" Iroha took off the PE jacket in a single motion.

The smell of flowers wafted about.

Under the jacket, she was wearing something reminiscent of an idol's or a game character's outfit. It was intricately ornate and brazenly exposing; the sight of her bare skin was dazzling.

Yahiro could not take his eyes off that embarrassing outfit, however. His face paled in pure shock and confusion.

"...Why are you wearing Waon's outfit...?"

"Because I'm Waon! I was in the middle of a stream when you guys got here!"

Iroha Waon turned out to be Iroha Mamana. His brain finally made the connection but refused to accept it. It didn't feel real.

Waon herself said she was a Japanese survivor and lived in Tokyo, but no one took her seriously. Iroha fit the bill, though. And seeing her up close, her face certainly looked like Waon's. She was just missing the silver hair and blue eyes, but it wasn't anything a wig and color contacts couldn't take care of. The deciding factor was her voice. It was literally the same as hers—strange that he only noticed now, even if he was hearing it live instead of through a speaker.

"Oh, wait! Yahiro... Are you...Yahiron?! No way!" Iroha pointed at him and shouted.

Yahiro wanted to curl up into a ball.

The girl in front of him had read all his messages. Just the thought of it had his face burning like lava.

Iroha's next reaction was far from what he expected, though. Huge tears started pouring from her eyes as she stared at him.

"What? Why're you crying?!" Yahiro's mind froze. He thought he was getting used to her sudden mood swings, but he could not possibly comprehend why she would start crying in that moment.

"I'm... I'm just so happy...," she replied between sobs, sniffling. "I was so scared... I thought there was not a single Japanese person out there watching my streams...but they reached someone... They reached you..."

Her voice trailed off at the end, but her feelings resonated with his.

Those streams were Iroha's way of testing the outside world safely, all while looking for a Japanese survivor. That was her reason for doing it despite the low viewership. As she went on for years, she naturally got anxious about it.

It turned out Yahiro was as much a ray of hope for her as she was for him. A strange feeling, for sure, but not a bad one.

"Let's move before the sun goes down. We must get as far away

from our pursuers as possible before going into uncharted territory. RMS won't be able to move at night, either," Yahiro told her after she calmed down.

There was much about the Moujuu's lifestyle that was still unknown, but Yahiro knew from experience that they were more active during the night. And even setting that aside, it was borderline suicidal trying to travel across a city in ruins without any light. They had to act quickly.

"I know... The kids are waiting for me, too." Iroha wiped her tears away and stood up.

She looked smaller and frailer than on camera, but he could see traces of Iroha Waon's face.

"To think the day would come when I saw *the* Iroha Waon's face all covered in tears and snot... I'm in shock, really."

"Shaddup. You should be glad you get to come in direct contact with your idol." Iroha laughed off Yahiro's poor attempt at lightening the mood. She immediately realized how that might have sounded and covered her chest. "Wait, but don't go touching me all of a sudden! No skin contact!"

"I'm not...touching you..." Yahiro suddenly felt all the strength leave his body as he retorted. His balance lost, he put a hand on the wall, but that still wasn't enough to keep him up. He couldn't move his limbs. As though it wasn't his body anymore. He sank into the deep, dark ocean of unconsciousness.

"Yahiro...?"

"No way... Not now... That damn backlash...!"

His immortal body lost all strength. It grew colder and colder. His skin turned pale like a corpse's. He suddenly lost the blessing—the toll of all the blood he'd shed.

"Yahiro?! What's wrong?! Stay with me, Yahiro! Yahiro!" Iroha screamed as she held him in her arms.

He felt the warmth of her touch as his senses began to vanish and all went dark.

3

"I hate it, Brother," the girl said as she turned.

It was a small girl in a brand-new sailor uniform. Her hair had gotten soaked in the sudden rain. Her face was shapely, still young. Her eyes were huge.

He'd seen this vision many times in his dreams. The image of a past he could never forget.

"I hate this whole world."

The sun peering in from between the clouds was nauseatingly red.

The cityscape seen from the rooftop was the same color.

The earth was awash in flames.

She extended her arms as she stood on the edge of the rooftop, the crimson fire as her background.

"Everything should just burn to the ground."

A dragon hovered behind the girl with the beautiful smile. It was a giant dragon with rainbow-hued wings.

He clenched his bloody fists and screamed within the dream.

†

Shortness of breath woke Yahiro up.

Something was on top of his face, blocking his vision. It felt like when your cats get on your bed on a chilly winter day. Heavy, but not uncomfortable. Through the cloth, he could smell the sweet scent of flowers and he felt a gentle warmth on his skin.

"Oh, sorry, are you awake?"

Yahiro's vision cleared as soon as he heard that.

Then he noticed his head was resting on a pair of thighs. Iroha's breasts had covered his eyes as she slouched.

"Ma...Mamana...?" He sat up, confused.

The feeling that something incredible had happened crossed his mind, but it was still hazy from waking up; he couldn't process it.

"What...was I...?"

He looked around. They were on the first floor of a half-wrecked office building. Right across was the convenience store they had rested at before he blacked out.

It was dark outside. The chilly night wind blew from the gaps in the crumbled walls.

"How many days was I out?!" he asked her, pale in the face.

Iroha jerked back in shock. "Days? It's been, like, three hours, I think..."

"Three hours? Really, that's all?" Yahiro shook his head, dumbfounded.

Iroha raised an eyebrow. She couldn't understand why he was so distressed.

"You just passed out all of a sudden. Are you okay?"

"Yeah... It's just the backlash from immortality. I lost too much blood today..." Yahiro pursed his lips, then sighed.

"Backlash?"

"Whenever I use my regeneration powers too much, I tend to black out. Then I usually end up sleeping for five days straight."

"Five days?!" Iroha's jaw was on the floor. "Then, if that happened while you were being attacked by Moujuu..."

"Yeah, my immortality's not as convenient as it sounds. I wouldn't need to be running around like this if I was *truly* invulnerable, don't you think?" He smiled wryly and sighed again.

Immortality's backlash—the cost of using those monstruous regeneration powers was the "death slumber."

Yahiro's body fell into sudden sleep periodically in order to compensate for the vitality lost from the wounds. It was a deep slumber, near to death, like suspended animation.

His body was completely defenseless in that condition. Not even he knew what would happen if he was killed in that situation, but considering his metabolism was stopped then, his body likely wouldn't be able to heal. The probability of him dying for good was quite high—so he wasn't entirely immortal.

"Then why?" Iroha asked, a serious look on her face.

Yahiro pushed his brows together, unable to understand the question. "Huh?"

"Why are you working as a salvager? You could faint out of nowhere…and never wake up again. So why?"

"Well, I–I…" He looked away and stammered.

In order to live. In order to earn money as efficiently as possible. There were many excuses he could make, but he didn't feel like lying.

Perhaps she really was concerned for him. In any case, he was definitely not opening up to her because he was thankful that she had let him sleep on her thighs.

"…Mamana, where were you when the J-nocide began?"

"Huh?" Iroha looked at him with suspicion.

Yahiro paid it no mind. "Official statements say the J-nocide was brought about by a meteorite. That the catastrophe caused by a meteorite in Tokyo triggered the J-nocide."

"A meteo…rite…?" Her expression turned stiff.

There was slight anger in her eyes. She understood what he'd meant with that question.

"No… That wasn't what I saw. It was no meteorite. A deep hole was opened right in the middle of Tokyo, but it wasn't a meteorite. That didn't summon the Moujuu." Her voice was trembling.

Yahiro nodded. "Yes. So you saw it, too." Yahiro smiled a creepy, hollow smile.

He could share the fear and despair he'd felt that day only with a fellow survivor.

No meteorite fell in Japan that day. It was something else that had brought about the J-nocide.

"It was…a dragon. A rainbow-colored dragon, so big that it covered the whole sky," Iroha said.

No one would believe them, no matter how hard they tried to explain it. A single dragon had wrecked the whole city. Iroha knew that.

So Yahiro kept the smile on his face.

"That was my sister."

"...Your sister?" She tilted her head, perplexed.

"I don't know if she summoned it or if it possessed her. But there is no doubt that she used the dragon's powers to try and make her wish come true."

"What...was her wish?"

"She wished for the world to end," he replied in a monotone.

It didn't feel real, putting it into words like that. Yet there was no denying the reality of the dragon's emergence and the crumbling of his peaceful life. It had granted her wish.

"So I...attacked her. I tried to kill Sui, my sister, with my own hands."

He clenched his right fist. The sensation of blood lingered on his hands. That illusion hadn't faded ever since that day.

"You're...kidding...right?" Iroha shook her head weakly.

Yahiro shrugged and chuckled.

"There's no greater proof than this ridiculous body of mine. I killed the dragon and bathed in its blood and became immortal. Ever heard of such a legend?"

Iroha was dumbstruck. She had seen both the dragon and Yahiro's healing powers with her own eyes. She had no way to argue against it.

"But, Yahiro, you said you were looking for your sister, right?" Weird thing to do if he had killed her.

"I failed." He grimaced.

"What do you mean?"

"I couldn't kill my sister. So I want to find her and kill her for good this time. I've been working as a salvager in order to gather funds to search for her. It's a well-paying job."

He spoke about it in such a detached manner; Iroha could only stare at him, astonished, not even blinking. Tears started flowing from her eyes all of a sudden.

"Hold on... Why are you crying...?"

"That's...that's just so sad! You want to kill your sister... You've been living all this time just to kill her! That's... I feel so sorry for you!" Iroha sobbed convulsively as she shook her head hard.

Why does she cry at the tiniest thing? Yahiro couldn't believe it. He was glad that she cared enough to cry for him, but to tell the truth, more than that, he found it annoying.

Yahiro had lived all by himself ever since the J-nocide; naturally, he didn't know how to handle girls his age. What was he supposed to say?

"Um, Mamana..."

"Don't call me that... I'm not your mama!"

"No, I'm just calling you by your name..."

Yahiro considered just ignoring her, but right then, he knew he could no longer worry about such silly things.

"Iroha, can you call a Moujuu?" he whispered while grabbing his sword.

"You mean...like Nuemaru? I've never tried it," she answered between sobs, realizing he had suddenly become serious.

"Oh." Yahiro bit his lip. He couldn't rely on a Moujuu to protect her or take her away.

"Why?" She wiped her face and stood up.

Yahiro glared through the crevices of the building and answered curtly. "The enemy's here."

4

The staff at the command room of the Japanese branch of Raimat International were reporting the situation in a frenzy.

"Lakhitov squad has located the Kushinada and her companion."

"We've sent all squads her location. I will bring up a city map."

A bird's-eye view of the city was displayed on the large monitors at the center of the room. It was a real-time feed of the 23 Wards from a drone flying eighteen kilometers in the air.

"Good thing the Moujuu don't notice drones flying in the stratosphere." Count Hector Raimat chuckled as he observed the images from where he sat in the base commander's seat.

The 23 Wards were a no-fly zone due to Moujuu attacks, but the drone at such high altitude had experienced no problems so far. Emphasis on these last two words, since a Moujuu with attack methods equal to a surface-to-air missile could very well appear in the future.

"Indeed. This is the maximum resolution image we could get, but I believe it is enough to guide our troops." A voice suddenly sounded from behind the count.

A young man clad in a gaudy uniform was just entering the command room. RMS Commander Firman La Hire.

"You're back, Major. How's your new arm doing?" The count glanced at Firman's right arm.

The hand peeking out from his uniform's sleeve was made of steel now.

"It is doing well. As we expected from the development of the Mod-3." Firman raised his artificial arm up to his eyes.

He had lost his right arm in combat against Yahiro Narusawa. A Fafnir soldier's healing ability wasn't enough to regenerate a lost limb.

Said healing abilities did close the wound immediately, however, which in turn made it impossible to reattach an organic arm. It was yet again the Fafnir soldier's power, though, that made his body conform to the new artificial arm in a matter of hours.

Firman's artificial arm, built for his draconized state, was twice as big as a regular human's. His grip strength exceeded two hundred kilograms, and his fingers were hard enough to pierce a bulletproof vehicle's armor.

"Good. Excellent," the count muttered, uninterested, before turning back to the monitor.

The drone above the 23 Wards was looking at the Chuo Ward and its surroundings. Or rather, the place that used to be the Chuo Ward.

There was no land where there once was, in a section of what used to be Chuo, Chiyoda, Minato, and Koto. In its place was only darkness. A giant bottomless pit right in the middle of Tokyo.

It was nearly three kilometers in diameter. The hole was covered in pitch-black miasma, through which not even state-of-the-art reconnaissance satellites could look. Not even echo-sounding or pulsed lasers worked.

The only thing anyone knew about it was that Moujuu came from there. It was their portal to the human world.

"The Ploutonion… It is incredible, no matter how many times I see it," the count muttered in awe.

The Ploutonion was the name for the hole at the 23 Wards' center.

"That hole is the scar of the Hollow Regalia?"

There was surprise in Firman's tone. The Ploutonion's existence was kept highly confidential; it was his first time seeing it.

"Yes. That is the portal to the underworld that Superbia, the earth dragon, gave birth to," the count answered with a serene smile.

The Ploutonion was connected to another world—this was the most widely accepted theory. It sounded unbelievable, but the Moujuu's supernatural abilities gave one no choice but to believe it. It was also said that the Ploutonion was created by a dragon.

"Don't you go thinking you can obtain the Hollow. No human can handle such a power. There is no better proof of that than the current state of the 23 Wards." The count warned Firman as he stared, bewitched by the Ploutonion.

"I understand." Firman apologized and straightened his posture.

The dragon had obliterated a capital city in a single night. Its powers as a weapon were extraordinary. But if one was to compare just on the scope of its destruction, then a nuclear weapon was enough.

Yet the risks of the dragon's powers went beyond a nuclear bomb's.

The land absorbed by the Ploutonion wasn't destroyed—it was transported, inhabitants and all, across world borders to another realm, leaving only a giant hole behind on this side.

Humanity didn't yet completely understand the effects of this hole on the world.

Would the portal one day close, Moujuu ceasing to emerge? Would it get larger little by little until it absorbed the whole world? Nobody knew.

"What we need is not the Regalia. We need a dragon's vessel," the count said.

"I will take care of that," Firman replied confidently.

The count nodded placidly. "Very well. How many men are in your pursuit troop?"

"Twelve Fafnir soldiers. I will add another twenty-four."

"Is that enough to defeat the Lazarus?" the count asked with suspicion, reproaching him between the lines for letting the boy get away once already.

Firman, oddly enough, recognized the uncertainty.

"If that is a real Lazarus we're dealing with, then no number of Mod-2 soldiers will be enough to kill him."

"Then what should we do?"

"We don't need to kill him. We simply have to keep attacking him without rest. We'll wear him down," Firman said with a callous smile.

He was openly stating he would sacrifice his thirty-six subordinates for that, yet no one present criticized him for it.

"Though immortal, he is human. There is no way he could keep on healing himself for eternity. And even if it turned out to be possible, there's no way his mind would be able to keep up."

"I see." The count smiled.

Death, in a sense, was salvation—liberation from all pain and suffering. To be the Lazarus was to be cursed and denied that salvation.

Under constant, incessant attacks and an endless infliction of pain, Yahiro Narusawa's mind would eventually go past its limits and break. It was the most reasonable strategy to use against the Lazarus.

"Although the short duration is, too, a defect among the Fafnir soldiers. It might be tricky if the Lazarus boy intends to stay in the 23 Wards," the count pointed out.

The excessive burden on the operators' bodies was the F-med's draconization's biggest flaw. One could keep draconization up for ten minutes max, though there were variations depending on the individual. And repeatedly undergoing draconization accelerated cellular deterioration and put a heavier load on internal organs, as well as producing various side effects.

None of this was communicated to the operators, of course. Fafnir soldiers were meant as sacrifices for short-term, decisive battles.

In any case, traveling across the Moujuu-infested 23 Wards without Fafnir soldiers was not possible. Were they to lose sight of their target or take too long to catch up to them, RMS could become exhausted first.

They were able to catch up to them only because Yahiro Narusawa had stopped moving for four hours, for whatever reason, but they couldn't expect things to go as well next time. Since they had no way to trail them other than drones, Raimat's top priority now was to figure out Yahiro Narusawa's escape route.

"About that, Count, we've received information from Galerie Berith," Firman said, trying to contain his grin.

The count raised his eyebrows. "Oh? That's unexpected. I thought you clashed back there during the mission."

"They did present a formal objection toward the fact that we tried to steal the Kushinada from them." Firman shook his head with an awkward smile on his face. "But they also apologized for their guide running away with her and stated they want to share her escape route with us."

"They...what?"

"Yes. The Kushinada plans to cross either Shibuya or Minato and head toward the Port of Yokohama."

"Yokohama... Interesting." The count stroked his chin.

The former territories of Shibuya and Minato were uncharted—dangerous zones full of high-Grade Moujuu.

There was no guarantee even the Fafnir soldiers could make their way through those areas; perhaps they thought that would be the safest route, considering the Kushinada's powers to control the Moujuu.

"Do you think we can trust them?" the count asked.

"There are no inconsistencies in what they've told us so far, at least. And I'm sure they wouldn't want to get on Raimat International's bad side." Firman put on a self-assured smile.

Fair judgment, the count thought.

"Still, I hesitate to send even Fafnir soldiers to uncharted territory."

"I agree, but if the Kushinada is heading toward Kanagawa, then she has few escape routes. She would have to cross the river in order to leave the 23 Wards."

"Are you saying we wait for them on the other side?" The count closed his eyes to think.

Firman's strategy was not reckless in the slightest. Quite the opposite, in fact: It sounded too good to be true. But even if what Galerie Berith said was false, they would only waste time and nothing else. It could even serve as an excuse to get rid of that pesky bunch.

"Very well. Tell the RMS main body in Sendai to roll out."

"Thank you, Count." Firman bowed in satisfaction.

The count looked at him emotionlessly and said, "Oh, and I also want you to capture the Lazarus boy, not just the Kushinada. Dead or alive." *If you can kill him, that is.*

Firman smiled ferociously.

"I swear on this arm, I will."

5

Yahiro was just a salvager, not a soldier. He wasn't prepared to take a human life. Thus, what he feared the most was to be told to surrender in peaceful negotiations. He wasn't heartless enough to attack someone who tried to talk things out.

But as soon as they found Yahiro out, the RMS operators attacked him. Yahiro was grateful; now he didn't have to over-think things.

There were four of them—all Fafnir soldiers. They were armed with knives instead of rifles, perhaps fearing a bullet might hit Iroha by mistake. Though close combat favored Yahiro.

He wasn't used to killing people. He didn't hesitate to counter in self-defense, but he didn't think himself capable of defeating professional killers.

However, his concerns were only against fighting humans. He had accumulated more experience than he could ever want killing Moujuu. And the way these Fafnir soldiers fought, they were more like beasts than humans.

"It's a shame, really." Yahiro cut down the first Fafnir soldier to attack.

A single cut, even if deep, was not enough to kill a Fafnir soldier, though—which Yahiro was fine with, since he didn't have to hold back.

"I know you wouldn't have made it all the way here without that drug, but still, you shouldn't have undergone that transformation."

The Fafnir soldier collapsed, slashed from shoulder to side.

The RMS operators were beyond Yahiro's combat skills, but their physical abilities had developed too quickly, and they were unable to control their own bodies. Yahiro might have been over-whelmed by their speed and power had they fought like humans, but their Moujuu-like motions were ubiquitous to the point of boredom.

Yahiro stayed calm even as three of them attacked simulta-neously from different directions. This was a common tactic among smaller Moujuu, and he knew well what to do in such instances.

"Wh-wha—?!" The fastest Fafnir soldier suddenly tumbled to the ground, his tough body deeply gouged by an invisible blade.

"It's just a wire, nothing out of this world. I figured you guys were fast enough to get hurt by this." Yahiro explained his strategy to restrict their movements. He walked through the web of wires planted indoors and cut down the trapped soldiers one by one.

He intentionally missed their vitals, but he slashed without restraint. Such wounds would still kill any normal human, but Fafnir soldiers were tougher than that. They would survive *if*they reached the outside and received proper treatment.

"Wretched Lazarus!"

The rearguard operators reached them and spotted their defeated colleagues. Yahiro noticed the guns in their hands and immediately used the Fafnir soldiers as shields. The rifles' bullets had high piercing force, but the soldiers' bodies were stronger; they absorbed the attack, disturbing their allies.

"Agh...!" The operators threw their guns away and took their F-meds.

Just as Yahiro wanted.

He hurled a hand grenade at the now-unarmed group; he had taken it from the first group of Fafnir soldiers.

The grenade exploded right between him and the rearguard group. Shards flew in all directions, and the Fafnir soldiers immediately got down to dodge them. During which time Yahiro closed the distance between them.

"Don't get so distracted. That barely does any damage to us, remember?"

The Fafnir soldiers' mouths went agape at the sight of the bloody boy. Their minds were still bound by common human sense—he made full use of his immortal body.

"Wait...don't!"

"Y'know, four years of fighting monsters do teach you a thing or two."

The soldiers shrieked, the idea of attacking back completely gone from their minds as Yahiro cut them down.

Less than three minutes later, Yahiro had defeated the total of twelve Fafnir soldiers, putting an end to the battle.

"Yahiro!" Iroha screamed the moment she saw him come back drenched in blood.

Most of it was his enemies', but he wasn't unharmed. Iroha took notice of this.

His wounds had already healed, however. His clothes were tattered after the grenade blast, but he just needed to change. And it wasn't that bad as far as Galerie Berith's coat was concerned; it was terribly dirty for sure, but the bulletproof, knife-proof uniform had maintained itself relatively well.

"You should see the other guys. Anyway, we should move along before another squad catches up," he replied calmly to keep her at ease.

He could no longer hear the engines of armored personnel carriers, but that only meant they were already nearby. They had to leave ASAP to avoid needless combat.

Iroha, though, stayed still, staring at the bloody man with fear.

"What do you mean? Did you…kill them?" Her voice was trembling.

Yahiro felt a sting in his chest. Iroha noticed his sour expression and raised her hands to her mouth. She realized her question had hurt him. She clung to him before he could even open his mouth to say something back.

"I'm sorry. I shouldn't have said that. I know you did it for my sake…"

"Oh, I'm not worried about it. Just keep your distance, okay? The blood's still fresh. It's gonna ruin your jacket."

"No. I won't let you go until you accept my apology." Iroha hugged him even harder, resisting against his push.

Weird way to throw a tantrum. Yahiro sighed with an awkward smile on his face.

"There's nothing for you to apologize for. I'm not mad. And I didn't kill them."

"You...didn't?"

"Can't you tell just looking at me? Those guys don't die so easily. I hurt them just enough so that they won't be getting up anytime soon."

The Fafnir soldier's healing ability was not nearly as great as the Lazarus's; he confirmed they wouldn't recover from a broken bone right away.

Leaving them disabled back there would still put them in danger of getting killed by Moujuu, naturally, but there were more troops on their way; they could take care of them. And while they were tending to the wounded, Yahiro and Iroha would have the time to escape. He'd thought all of this up when deciding not to kill them.

"Got it? Good. Now, let's run. Their reinforcements are right around...the corner..." Yahiro gulped as he saw what was going on beyond the crumbled walls.

RMS's operators were approaching the wounded Fafnir soldiers according to plan. What they did to them, though, was beyond his imagination. They took out cylinders filled with crimson liquid and stabbed them into their colleagues' bodies. An extra dose of F-med.

"What the...? Why aren't they taking them back?! They're gonna make them fight like that?!" Yahiro was disturbed by their actions.

The extra dose had dramatic effects on the soldiers. Their bodies swelled and doubled in size, and their wounds were healed in the blink of an eye.

However, many of them were not able to handle it. The sudden multiplication of their cells made their bodies collapse in on themselves, blood and flesh bursting all around.

"So they don't care about anyone unable to fight?!" Yahiro ground his teeth.

RMS operators didn't see each other as comrades, only fellow workers with the same goal. They would make use of one another to the very end and then discard their colleagues when no use remained.

"Yahiro…it's over. We're surrounded!" Iroha yelled as she looked at the building's entrance.

The other RMS squad had surrounded the building while their attention was on the wounded Fafnir soldiers.

"Iroha, go hide upstairs," Yahiro instructed her as he turned to glance at the stairway.

"What about you?" she asked with a stiff expression.

"Don't worry. I'll take care of this quickly."

"Yahiro…?!" She tried to stop him, but the unsheathing of his sword shut her up.

The RMS operators came crashing into the building at the same time.

The first to attack were the four Fafnir soldiers dosed with extra F-med. They were controlled by their offensive instincts— coordinating with one another as members of a squad was no longer possible. They didn't even unsheathe their knives; they jumped at Yahiro using their claws.

They were much faster than before. As soon as he countered one, another attacked. He couldn't dodge that.

"Ugh…!"

Yahiro was thrown backward, a deep gouge in his side. The soldiers seized the opportunity. Yahiro countered reflexively and injured a second one badly, but the other rampaging soldiers stopped at nothing. Noticing he wouldn't be able to dodge the next attack, he dug into the third foe's torso while accepting the damage to himself. He then sacrificed his left shoulder as he neutralized the last one.

"–?!" Yahiro grunted in pain as he escaped the Fafnir soldiers' encirclement, and bullets rained down all around him.

It was the reinforcement troop. They got both of his legs, and he fell to the debris-strewn floor. New Fafnir soldiers rushed in.

The midrange guns and the Fafnir soldiers attacked in waves. RMS didn't seem intent on defeating him in one go anymore; they were trying to wear him down over time now, deplete his stamina at a tremendous pace. They knew his weakness. He could fall into the death slumber once again if this battle went on.

Panicked, Yahiro unconsciously soaked his blade in his own blood. There was no reason for this. He simply did it out of habit after years spent fighting Moujuu.

A Fafnir soldier clawed at Yahiro's head, where he still lay on the floor. He quickly turned his body and swung his katana as he stood up.

The strange position reduced the power of his attack. The Fafnir soldier's tough scales repelled his blade; he managed only a shallow cut on his right arm.

He could not believe what happened next, however. The soldier's right arm started creaking, instantaneously bulging and growing multiple times its size.

"Gwaaah!!" the Fafnir soldier shrieked. His draconized face twisted in pain, his face corroding from within.

His healing went out of control. His body cells multiplied endlessly until he could no longer keep his form. His mass tripled, at which point he burst like a balloon. Blood plasma rained over Yahiro as he stared dumbfounded at what had just occurred.

His blood had devastated the Fafnir soldier. His blood-covered Kuyo Masakane coming in contact with the Fafnir soldier's modified body had produced this abnormal activity in his cells.

"What in the...? They're like Moujuu...?" Yahiro muttered as he looked down at the lumps of what used to be the soldier.

The Lazarus's blood was poison to the Moujuu, but why would it have a similar effect on the Fafnir soldiers, too?

The effect on the Fafnir soldiers was decidedly different from the Moujuu's, however. The latter simply crumbled away. Meanwhile, the former saw their bodies activated in an abnormal manner. As though they were overdosing on F-med. Or like some sort of anaphylactic shock.

"Fafnir... Right... Why didn't I realize before?! Raimat...!" Yahiro's lips trembled in rage.

He kept on walking forward, defenseless. The Fafnir soldiers flinched for a second, in reaction to the overwhelming, ghastly aura pouring out of him.

The operators on the rear guard shot at him. He did not dodge. He kept on walking toward the enemy as bullets burrowed into his body.

The operators should have realized by then—he had unleashed the Lazarus's true power. He gave up on fighting like a human.

"Listen up, RMS operators! You've *got* to throw away that messed-up drug and run far from here! You *will* die!" Yahiro warned them, but his voice was drowned out by the gunfire.

One of the Fafnir soldiers tried attacking him from behind, but then, all of a sudden, he exploded, leaving only a painful howl behind. Then another went through the same. Then another. The Fafnir soldiers' bodies went berserk as soon as they even approached Yahiro.

The gunners got fed up with their weapons' uselessness and all took out cylinders full of crimson liquid. Yahiro watched with disdain as they injected the drug into their bodies, then sighed.

All remaining operators turned into Fafnir soldiers. A total of thirty. Only thirty.

"So we're doing this... I'm not holding back, then, fellow monsters." Yahiro took off his Galerie coat.

He bared his upper body, a metallic shine peeking from the gaps of his tattered shirt. It was a dull glint, reminiscent of rusted armor. A scale armor—Yahiro's body had transformed, taking on the appearance of the cursed, immortal monster. The steel body of that legendary dragon slayer.

"Begone. There's no place for us in this world."

Yahiro's rusted, steel skin–covered face twisted into a vicious grin.

The massacre began.

6

"It's fine—don't be scared. We're leaving now, okay?" Iroha smiled as she reached out to pet the golden beast's fur.

A giant monster stood in front of her, about eight meters in length. A winged beast with the head of a lion, like the mythological Anzû. A Grade-IV Moujuu found near the uncharted territory.

"Yes, who's a good boy? You're a good boy. I'll see you later." Iroha caressed the monster that could easily bite her in half like it was nothing.

The golden Moujuu, satisfied, flapped its wings and returned to its nest.

"Oof, that was nerve-racking. Speaking to strangers gets my heart racing." Iroha wiped the sweat from her forehead and heaved a heavy sigh.

"Usually, your heart stops beating the moment you meet a Grade-IV Moujuu, so hey," Yahiro replied as he stared aghast at Iroha's giggling profile.

They were currently near the Ohi Racecourse, moments away from entering the Ohta Ward—out of the unexplored zone.

They had encountered fifteen large Moujuu on their way there. All of them were powerful enough to obliterate a whole battalion, but Iroha had won them all over and sent them away. The sight of it reminded Yahiro of how incredible her power was.

The power of the Kushinada, able to freely control the Moujuu. Once her powers were analyzed, humanity could hope to get rid of the threat inside the 23 Wards...and perhaps even weaponize the Moujuu. No wonder Raimat International—top arms dealer—was so obsessed with getting their hands on her.

Such thoughts on his mind, Yahiro approached the bike he had parked on the street. An off-road bike for motocross, Japanese-made. He had taken it from a store's ruins.

The bike was in good shape despite four years of neglect; he'd only had to give it quick servicing, and the engine started right away. It was an old model, with a kick-start lever and no fuel injection, but that turned out to be fortunate for them. It was thanks to this bike that they were able to cross the uncharted territory in a single night after defeating the RMS troops.

Yahiro got on it and restarted the engine clumsily, still unused to the kick-start lever. They were less than ten kilometers from the Tama River, the prefecture border. They would be able to get out of the 23 Wards before sunrise if nothing unexpected happened.

"Man... It's like we're in a teen movie, huh?" Iroha spoke from the back seat, holding her hair away from her eyes as it whipped in the wind.

The seat of the competitive bike was cramped, so she had to sit glued to Yahiro's back.

The roads were wrecked and full of obstacles, so he had to keep the speed down to bicycle level; this made it easier to talk, in turn.

"A teen movie?"

"Yeah, but like the romantic kind. You know, the honor-student pretty girl runs away with the delinquent boy on his bike."

"You calling me a delinquent?" Yahiro frowned. He refrained from commenting on her boldness in calling herself a *pretty girl*.

"You still worried about how you couldn't save the Fafnir soldiers' lives?" she asked, leaning on his back.

Yahiro was caught off guard; he stayed quiet.

He'd ultimately had to kill all the RMS operators he had fought last night. The Fafnir soldiers could not even touch him; they'd all exploded.

They did that to themselves by ignoring his warning not to use the F-med, but still, he'd ended up taking thirty lives. Iroha guessed he was disheartened because of it. And he did take comfort in her phrasing. He'd wanted to save their lives, help them. They were only victims just as he was, and he hadn't wanted them to die.

"...It was Sui's blood," Yahiro muttered.

He felt Iroha's confusion from behind. "Sui?"

"That so-called F-med they're using...it's Sui's blood."

"You mean your sister's? Your long-lost sister's?"

"I should've realized sooner. The way they look, that ridiculous healing power...it's the same power as mine. Raimat's using dragon blood to create his own immortal army!" Yahiro exclaimed in a low voice.

The crimson liquid was a product of Sui Narusawa's blood. Dragon blood that gave the power of immortality to those who bathed in it. But it had its side effects—it was poison to incompatible subjects. That was why the Fafnir soldiers' regenerative ability went out of control when overdosing on F-med.

In order to control the side effects, they chemically processed the dragon blood, limiting the duration of its efficacy. Thus the F-med was born. This explained why they underwent intense anaphylactic shock when they came in contact with Yahiro's blood. His was much more densely polluted with dragon blood than they were used to.

Raimat was using dragon blood as a weapon. As incredible as it might sound, this implied something even bigger: Raimat International had access to enough dragon blood to mass-produce the F-med. Access to Sui Narusawa's blood.

"You mean Raimat's got Sui captive?"

"Most likely. I can't think of any other way they'd be able to get so much of her blood." Yahiro nodded at Iroha's question.

Firman La Hire had his own special, improved version of the F-med—Mod-3. This implied they had been researching dragon blood for many years already.

In order to get enough to research the F-med and to mass-produce it, they needed a steady flow of blood from a living dragon—impossible if they didn't have one captive.

"...Wait. Raimat's the sponsor of your clients, isn't it?" Iroha's voice turned tight as she realized something.

Yahiro nodded in silence. Raimat International was indeed the sponsor of Operation: Kushinada Hunt–they had hired Galerie Berith.

"Giuli and Rosé, were they? Did Galerie Berith know about Raimat having a hold on Sui?"

"Probably. Though maybe they didn't know it was her blood that was used on the F-med... No, they surely did if they knew about her."

Yahiro remembered the picture of Sui the twins had shown him. She was on a coffin-like bed, tubes connected everywhere to her body. The machines surrounding her likely weren't just for life support–they were for extracting her blood.

Iroha wasn't entirely convinced even then.

"That's weird, though... They were supposed to tell you where she was for helping them out, right? Then they would've known from the very beginning that you'd go against Raimat."

"I guess they hired me to ultimately reduce Raimat's forces. Those two companies might be working together this time, but they're competitors. It makes sense," he replied flatly.

Iroha's voice turned more serious. "Yes, it makes sense. Which is what makes it weird."

"What?"

"If they wanted to have you fight Raimat, then why would they let us go? It doesn't make sense to let you escape now."

"Oh..." Yahiro couldn't say anything back.

They were on their way to Yokohama under Galerie Berith's twins' instructions, in order to escape from Raimat's pursuit coming from Saitama. The instruction itself was reasonable. Crossing the uncharted territory did in fact stop RMS's pursuit. But this also meant that RMS would see no losses, either. It didn't make sense if their ultimate goal was to have Yahiro fight Raimat.

"Well, wouldn't it be so they can get their hands on you?"

It made sense if they prioritized getting Iroha over attacking Raimat, but Iroha immediately denied the notion.

"Then why wouldn't they come right for us? Don't you think making us two cross the unexplored area all alone could only be risky?"

"I knew something was off about them from the start," Yahiro said with regret.

Iroha's remark was plausible. There was no need to tell them to run if they wanted him to fight Raimat. And if they just wanted Iroha, they shouldn't have shown him Sui's picture. Galerie Berith's actions were contradictory. The twins were scheming something.

"We have no choice but to go, though, even if they're tricking us. Your kids are waiting for you."

Yahiro decided that there was no point in doubting further. There was nothing else they could do anyway.

"*Siblings!* They're not my children!" Iroha corrected him.

Silence fell. Iroha breathed deeply a couple of times in an unusual display of hesitation; then she decided to confess what was on her mind.

"Hey, Yahiro. I have something to apologize to you for."

"Uh-oh… Did you do something to me while I was sleeping?" he asked with suspicion.

Iroha opened her eyes wide. "What're you thinking about?! Of course not! I wouldn't do that!"

"C'mon, I was just joking…"

"Sh-shaddup!" Her voice turned shrill as she hit his back repeatedly.

Yahiro was confused as to why that would get her so flustered.

"So what is it? Apologize for what?"

"Um… I think I met Sui before the J-nocide."

"What?!"

Yahiro hit the brakes, making the bike stand on its front wheel for a second.

"Eep! What's wrong with you?! Don't stop all of a sudden! You want to kill us?!"

Iroha clung to Yahiro's back, desperately trying not to go flying. He turned around to look at her.

"Forget that—what did you just say?! You met Sui?! When?! Where?!"

"In...my dreams...?" she answered uneasily, feeling overwhelmed.

"In your dreams?"

Yahiro was utterly confused. He didn't feel she was pranking him or anything, but he didn't understand what she was getting at. He furrowed his brow as he stared at her, but then his expression stiffened.

"Looks like we're gonna have to continue this conversation later."

"Yahiro?" Iroha followed his gaze and turned around, then gasped.

The sun was about to rise over the city ruins; the landscape all around was full of fallen buildings—destroyed in explosions—and scorched earth.

Far on the level horizon was a group of dully glowing armored vehicles. About twelve tanks and countless operators were waiting to encircle Yahiro and Iroha. They all wore lavish uniforms reminiscent of medieval nobles—RMS.

"An ambush?!" Iroha exclaimed, mouth agape.

There was no way RMS could have followed them through the uncharted territory. And even if they had, they shouldn't have been able to gather such a large troop ahead of them.

There was only one possible explanation: They knew the pair was heading to Yokohama. Someone had leaked their escape route to RMS. And who else but...?

"Galerie Berith... The twins sold us out..."

Yahiro's shoulders trembled in anger as he beat the bike's handle. RMS's armed troops immediately surrounded them.

7

The tank shell soared overhead and burst behind them.

The explosion gouged the road, pieces of asphalt raining all around. They didn't miss the shot—they actually hit their mark. Their goal was to block Yahiro and Iroha's escape route.

"Iroha, you've gotta surrender!" Yahiro exclaimed amid the explosion.

The Galerie twins were not there; Raimat had shown up instead.

The leak could hardly be called betrayal. Yahiro was nothing but their contractor, a mere guide. It was only natural they could cut him off without thought. It was much more beneficial to Galerie Berith to sell Yahiro over to get on Raimat's good side, rather than recklessly oppose them to get their hands on Iroha.

He was used to being tricked just for being Japanese. Or so he thought. He realized he had unconsciously trusted the twins. He gritted his teeth.

"Surrender...? You want me to go with them?" Iroha was clearly upset.

RMS was her enemy—the ones who had destroyed her home and killed her family.

"They want your powers, so they shouldn't treat you harshly. I'm sure you could get them to talk with the Galerie and get your siblings back, too." Yahiro tried hard to convince her.

Taking her with him and surviving this situation was impossible. It was better for her to surrender before getting harmed.

Reality did not give him hope for that, however. The ground at their feet burst. Assault-rifle shots blew the bike away in a rain of sparks.

"?!"

Yahiro pushed Iroha to the ground to protect her from the incoming fire. A few shots grazed him, causing blood to spill from his shoulder.

They hit his trapezius. Part of his shoulder blade was shattered. It would take only about ten seconds to heal, but he wouldn't be able to keep Iroha safe if the bullets hit him cleanly.

"What're you trying to do?! Didn't you come here for the Kushinada?!" Yahiro yelled at the shooters as he stood up despite the pain.

The RMS operators were positioned atop the rubble along the road. There were about fifteen of them. At the center was Firman La Hire, now sporting a big artificial arm.

"Oh, we will capture her. It's just, no one said she had to be unharmed."

Firman ordered his underlings to fire another round of warning shots.

Bullets rained around Iroha; asphalt shards hit her. She did not scream even then, only glaring at Firman with burning ire.

"It wouldn't be a good look for me to have you surrender immediately after gathering this many men. Give them something to do for a little while, at least."

His underlings snickered in response.

The warning shots were getting closer and closer to hitting them. Japanese survivors with supernatural powers must be no different from Moujuu to them. They had killed many of their colleagues, too—no reason for them to feel guilty about harming the pair.

Yahiro would have had a better chance of winning had they used the F-med. He had no way of standing against un-draconized, gun-wielding humans.

"I see... This is what you want... To keep me in one place!" Yahiro gritted his teeth at the realization.

They kept on firing warning shots at Iroha in order to stop Yahiro from taking action. She could be in danger if he made a move, and the mere thought kept him stuck in place.

Then their next move should be...

"—!"

Firman drew a handgun with his left hand. He aimed at Yahiro's heart and shot right away. Yahiro stopped the bullet with his right arm. Sparks popped off, and the bullet bounced away as fresh blood armor covered his skin.

"Oh, I get it. Lazarus...you bathed in dragon blood. That is how you got the Sigurd body! An armor no steel can harm!" Firman's lips contorted in exhilaration; all the while, he kept on shooting at Yahiro.

Yahiro's blood armor was supposed to be his last resort–something he hadn't shown even Galerie Berith. But the situation called for its use. The bullet would have hit Iroha had he dodged instead. Firman had chosen that angle on purpose.

"Marvelous! Oh, so excellent! This goes beyond the Mod-2! The count will be elated once I deliver you to him alive!"

Firman threw his gun away now that its magazine was empty and picked up a bigger weapon from the ground instead. A six-barrel machine gun. The electric Gatling gun was able to shoot the ridiculous amount of six thousand shots per minute. It was the kind of weapon equipped to military helicopters, and Firman was holding it with one hand–something possible only thanks to his Fafnir-soldier strength on top of the artificial arm's power.

"Yet I still can't stop my right arm from doing this!"

Firman fired the machine gun. He pulled the trigger for only a single moment, and in that blink of an eye, dozens of bullets flew at Yahiro with incredible accuracy.

"Guh?!"

Yahiro's body was blown back, his blood armor shattered. Not even the dragon blood's steel body could stop such a great quantity of bullets. The power of modern technology slammed him to the ground, yet his form remained human even then, not so much thanks to the blessings of his Lazarus's body but due to Firman deliberately avoiding fatally harming him.

"Yahiro! Yahiro!!" Iroha stood up and spread her arms, covering for the boy on the ground.

Two Fafnir soldiers ran up to her and pinned her down right away. She did not resist as they took her away from Yahiro.

Once the boy was free, Firman pulled the trigger again, blowing Yahiro away as he tried to rise and ripping his left arm off in the process.

"Ha-ha! You still live no matter how many times I shoot at you! Impressive, Lazarus!"

Firman no longer aimed. He shot a haphazard curtain of bullets, shredding Yahiro into bits and pieces of meat. Nothing stopped him; he pulled the trigger even harder with each sign of healing, as though testing the limits of the Lazarus.

"How much blood have you shed up to now, though? How much dragon blood do you have left in your body?!"

"No! Stop it! Let him go! Yahirooo!!" Iroha wailed, her hair in total disarray.

Yahiro remained on the ground. His appearance was still barely that of a human, but there were no signs of regeneration starting again. It looked as though Firman was right—he had bled too much.

Firman grinned in satisfaction then, but in the following moment, his smile was replaced with shock.

"Stop hurting hiiim!"

The Fafnir soldiers released Iroha all of a sudden. Free from their grip, she ran to Yahiro and covered him with her own body.

Firman immediately pulled his hand away from the trigger, but the machine gun shot at a rate of one hundred bullets per second—the short moment before he stopped was still enough to riddle Iroha with bullets. Her blood rained down on Yahiro.

"Y-you stupid broad!" Firman clicked his tongue as he threw away the machine gun.

The weapon was prepared for use against the Lazarus; its power was too much too devastating to be used against humans. Even the slightest brush of its fire would mean certain death. There was no way Iroha Mamana could survive this.

Firman directed his wrath toward the two Fafnir soldiers who had so easily let her go to her death, but the moment his glare fixed upon them, his eyes widened instead, and he gasped.

The two dragonmen were spaced out, staring at the fallen Iroha. Both their bodies were on fire.

Raging blue flames enveloped the Fafnir soldiers' bodies, turning them into pure-white ash. Their healing powers were far behind the fire's intensity. They soon burned up without any sound, leaving no trace.

"What...? What in the...? What in the world is going on?" Firman trembled.

It wasn't only the Fafnir soldiers' bodies on fire. Iroha's corpse above Yahiro was burning, too. The dazzling flames swirled fiercely like a vortex up to the sky—a giant dragon ascending to the skies.

"Fire! Shoot that woman's corpse! Stop the flames!" Firman yelled out of instinctive fear.

All operators pulled their triggers at once, and Firman, too, grabbed his machine gun.

The bullets, however, did nothing to harm Iroha's or Yahiro's bodies. The flames melted them away instantaneously, making them vanish before they reached the couple.

"This can't be...!" Firman's shapely face contorted horribly.

Then, like a trigger for disaster, the sound of a giant explosion shook the ruined city.

The armored vehicles behind Firman and his men exploded with a sonic boom.

The shot came from a cannon, main battle tank–class. The vehicles were built for protection against antipersonnel weaponry—their light armor stood no chance against anti-tank, high-velocity, armor-piercing bullets.

The vehicles were blown away along with nearby operators, and more shots came flying to destroy more vehicles before the first explosion even cooled down.

Following shots came from the skies, and by then the RMS troops were already in a state of panic. The group was unable to respond to the surprise attack, and some of the operators ran for their lives.

"Now what?!" Firman yelled at his subcommander.

The man, equipped with a data-link visor for infantry tactics, forced the voice out of his dry lips:

"W-we're under attack!"

"I can tell as much! Where's it coming from?!"

"From the overpass. It's an armored train! Galerie Berith's Yáo Guāng Xīng!"

"Galerie...Berith...?" Firman turned around, eyes wide in disbelief.

RMS's troops were deployed around the former Dai-Ichi Keihin highway, and the railroad ran parallel to it. There was a gray train on it: an eight-car armored train. The ironclad cars were all equipped with countless cannons, but the most surprising of all were the four big ones at the ends of the train. Smoothbore cannons, 55 caliber, 120mm. One car had the firepower of a platoon's main battle tank.

"They're going after us?! Was this their aim all along, luring in RMS's main troop to annihilate it?! The Lazarus and the Kushinada were nothing but bait?!" Firman was aghast.

The J-nocide had devastated Japan's traffic network, but the railroad lines alone maintained part of their functions, even up within some zones of the 23 Wards. Galerie Berith took advantage of this to mobilize their armored train in secret and launch a surprise attack on RMS.

The landscape of the ruined city–free of barriers and with the railway so close to the highway–was also perfect for such an attack. Galerie Berith had purposefully leaked Yahiro Narusawa's escape route to Firman in order to lure RMS there.

"Is this supposed to be payback for what I did during Operation: Kushinada Hunt? Foolish." Firman's voice was cool, but his ire was too hot to hide entirely.

The loss of the armored vehicles was great, but they still had the F-med. There were eight Fafnir soldiers still alive, including Firman himself–enough to subdue Galerie Berith's armored train.

Firman ordered his men to take the F-med. The Mod-3 version. This upgrade, on top of further elevating their power, also extended the time they could keep fighting. They needed a boost for the situation.

The draconized operators roared. Galerie Berith's train's antipersonnel machine guns were no longer a threat to the Fafnir soldiers. Firman took a deep breath to command the counterattack, but then he froze.

He saw a wavering silhouette rise inside the raging blue fire.

It was a young man, drenched in blood, carrying an unconscious girl.

Yahiro Narusawa, unsheathed katana in hand.

8

"Waooon! Hi, everywaon!"

Yahiro heard a nostalgic voice from inside his hazy mind. Iroha's. *I must be dreaming*, he thought.

A blue glow dazzlingly enveloped everything. He couldn't even see himself. He couldn't tell if he was floating or falling.

He knew only that Iroha was there. She was in a bare state beside him, but he could feel only her presence.

"I'm sorry, Yahiro. I just didn't know anything about myself..."

Iroha's thoughts flew into his mind. Her sadness, her grief, her worries, her regrets, her love. Her warm emotions gushed into Yahiro's wounded soul.

"I finally remember what happened that day..."

Endless fragments of memories popped into Yahiro's head.

A blue sky. A sea of clouds. Wings of fire. The sprawling city and vast sea extending below. A light.

A giant eight-headed dragon attending eight girls.

Yahiro then realized Iroha was standing before his eyes, naked. She was holding a sword tight to her chest.

Iroha raised the sword enveloped in flames and pointed it at Yahiro's heart.

Her sorrow escaped her in tears of blood falling onto Yahiro's chest.

"There was more than one dragon..."

†

"What're you doing coming into my dreams and shouting *Waooon* first thing?" Yahiro said languidly as he lay Iroha softly on the ground.

Her body was unharmed despite the shower of bullets. Her beloved PE jacket was torn to shreds, but her bare skin peeking from below it showed no injury.

He understood now why that was—no human attack could possibly harm her.

"You've gone too far, Firman La Hire."

Yahiro's body emerging from the flames was not that of a human or a dragonman—it was stranger, freakish.

His armor of dragon scales, like a cracked shell, covered his entire body now. Its lustrous surface glowed with the reflection of the wavering fire.

The blade of his katana was healed, too, no longer chipped by the previous shooting.

Yahiro held tight the bare shaft of the Kuyo Masakane, its *koshirae* sword sling already destroyed.

The Fafnir soldiers shook in their boots at the sight of his calm approach.

"I give you permission to attack of your own accord. There's no need to kill him. Rip his limbs off," Firman ordered his men.

"Roger…!" The Fafnir soldiers unsheathed their machetes, suppressing their fear.

Firman lifted his artificial right arm and unleashed the claws equipped to its fingertips.

Not even the barrage of bullets from that machine gun could kill the Lazarus; there was no need to kill him, then. They only had to paralyze and capture him, then put him on ice or something. Firman's plan was completely flawed, however.

"It's time for revenge!" Yahiro exclaimed to his katana.

The Fafnir soldiers slashed at him. He countered with amateurish motions, far below the refinement of the trained operators. There was no strategy in his attacks, no care for defense or even reach. He moved like a beast—which was the optimal battle style for the Lazarus. But how many of his opponents realized?

"Wha…?!" The subcommander gasped from behind Firman.

Two Fafnir soldiers exploded upon contact with Yahiro. Their regenerative ability went berserk, and they burst from the inside. Two more who rushed forward were immediately defeated as well.

The Fafnir soldiers' attacks did land, but their machetes stood no hope against Yahiro's armor; meanwhile, the slightest brush of his katana immediately killed the soldiers.

This was no battle. It was one-sided annihilation. The tables had turned in the blink of an eye. It was Firman and his men being hunted now.

"Cowards! Don't run! This is against your contract!"

His un-draconized subcommander and other men ignored Firman's orders and fled.

It was not only them—even the armored corps Galerie Berith was attacking began their retreat.

The Fafnir soldiers attacked Yahiro out of instinctive fear rather than following orders, but they quickly fell to the enraged Lazarus's blade.

Now only Firman remained.

"They were contractors. 'Course they'd run as soon as things got ugly," Yahiro told Firman with composure. There was even a bit of empathy in his voice, and this only made Firman angrier. "Oh, but I'm not letting you go, Major La Hire. I've got some questions to ask you."

"Yahiro Narusawaaa!" Firman charged toward him, claws in position.

Yahiro received the attack with his bare hand. Firman's steel arm with Fafnir strength had the power of a giant war hammer—not something a human body could stand.

Still, Yahiro's arm did not break. Firman noticed his astounding healing powers regenerated his body right before it was crushed.

Yahiro swung the katana in his right hand upward. Firman dodged the Fafnir soldier–slaying slash by throwing himself to the ground. It wasn't the time to care about appearances.

"How, Yahiro Narusawa?! You were already on the verge of

death!" Firman groaned bitterly, his face twisted in humiliation. Then he saw Iroha behind Yahiro. "I see—it was the Kushinada... She's...she's the same as Superbia...!"

Firman dashed forward, taking Yahiro by surprise. He headed for Iroha, who still lay on the ground.

Then Yahiro realized he intended on running away with her. The Fafnir soldier's speed was greater than even the Lazarus's. He wouldn't be able to catch up if he let him go.

And yet, despite knowing all this, Yahiro was oddly calm and collected.

He knew what he had to do. The sword inside him knew.

"Stop, Firman La Hire!" Yahiro gave his last warning, holding his katana tight.

He pictured a ray of light tearing open the darkness. A crimson glow burning the skies.

The flaming sword in Iroha's arms.

His whole body became a fiery torrent. Dragon-scorching fire. The power he hadn't been able to obtain that day four years ago.

The word left his lips without effort:

"Blaze."

One moment stretched into eternity. The distance between him and his enemy shortened to zero. The blade bolted to scorch the dragon blood—the diluted blood of Sui Narusawa flowing through the Fafnir soldier's body.

Yahiro was more than thirty feet away. He covered the massive distance impossibly quickly, then turned gracefully. Behind him was the last of the soldiers, engulfed in flames.

"This...can't be... I...I can't lose to this...monster..." Firman fell to the ground with a deep wound to his midsection before he could counterattack. The flames around his body intensified, quickly cremating him to white ash. "You...cursed monster..." Those were his final words right before his body vanished entirely.

Yahiro stared in silence.

He felt no sympathy. The man had shot him dozens, if not hundreds of times and had even tried to kill Iroha. Still, he couldn't help but think that, were it not for the dragon, he wouldn't have seen this end.

The crimson scales covering Yahiro's whole body came off one by one. Simultaneously, he felt the great raging power within him fading out. It was as though his body was silently telling him that there was no more dragon blood left for him to burn.

"Yahiro... You're...alive?"

He heard Iroha get up behind him. He turned around and, immediately, felt something soft push against him. She had run and crashed into him, clinging to him as tears endlessly ran down her cheeks.

"Thank goodness...you're okay..."

"I'm not. Why'd you go and do that?"

I'm the one who should be crying, geez. Yahiro sighed.

Just remembering the moment Iroha was shot while he was down paralyzed him with despair.

"I would also appreciate if you could give me some personal space. And, uh, do something about your clothing."

"...Wh-what do you— *Whoa?!*"

Iroha shrieked upon looking down and seeing her dark-red jacket torn to shreds. The live-stream outfit she was wearing underneath had been skimpy to begin with, but now it was crossing the line. Yahiro was also clearly jittery about their bare skin touching.

"D-did you see?" She glanced up at him while covering her chest.

"Nope," he replied bluntly.

Iroha looked annoyed. "You're lying! Why're you so red in the face, then?"

"That's just the morning sun." He averted his eyes to the east.

The sun was beginning to rise, dyeing the city ruins the color of blood.

RMS's armored corps were destroyed, and the surviving operators had already vanished. Its attack finished, Galerie Berith's armored train sat silently in the distance.

Then a girl with orange highlights scurried between Yahiro and Iroha.

"Whew, you two have become so close in such a short amount of time. Did something fun happen last night?"

"Eek!"

"Giuli?! Get outta here!"

Iroha shrieked while still covering her chest, while Yahiro raised his fists reflexively.

Giulietta Berith had popped up out of nowhere, but she showed no ill intention. Quite the opposite, she stared at Yahiro's katana with gleaming eyes like a curious child's.

"Hey, whazzat?! What'd you just do back there?! You were all like, *Fwsh*!!"

"Um...," Yahiro mumbled.

Giuli seemed to be referring to the way he'd slashed Firman, but not even Yahiro remembered how he did that. He had just felt that he could. He wasn't sure he'd be able to do it again.

"Is that your Regalia, Yahiro? Quite impressive. That Goreclad, too," said the blue-haired girl dispassionately from where she stood beside Giuli.

Regalia. Goreclad. Yahiro frowned; he didn't know those words.

"Rosé... What're you plotting? Why'd you appear here now?"

"No 'thank you'? We came here to rescue you," Rosetta Berith replied flatly, not particularly offended.

Yahiro pursed his lips in irritation. "You used us as bait, and now you want us to thank you?"

"Well, we got rid of most of RMS's forces thanks to that," Rosé replied unapologetically.

Her response left Yahiro at a loss for words.

"This means Raimat's defenses are down," Giuli said with an aggressive smile, like that of a cruel cat.

"No way... Are you...? Is this what you were aiming for all along?" Yahiro's voice cracked.

Galerie Berith knew that Raimat had Sui Narusawa captive and that Yahiro wanted to kill her.

There was no avoiding battle with Raimat in order to kill Sui Narusawa. And they were a massive military corporation. Not an enemy Galerie Berith could stand against.

However, after losing RMS's main forces, their PMC division would fall into chaos. By using them as bait, the twins had given him the chance to kill Sui Narusawa.

Yahiro stared astonished at the beautiful doll-like twins. They saluted him respectfully.

"Allow us to reintroduce ourselves. My name is Giulietta Berith, and this is my sister, Rosetta. We are here on behalf of the head of House Berith to receive you two."

Yahiro and Iroha were taken aback by Giuli's polite speech. Her expression was completely serious, however—it was no joke.

"Two? You mean Yahiro and me?"

"Indeed, Lady Iroha Mamana—or should I say, Avaritia, the fire dragon?"

"Ava... Avari-what?" Iroha tilted her head in confusion.

"So it wasn't Iroha's powers that you wanted?" Yahiro looked at them with suspicion.

He wasn't about to forget they had used them as bait in order to cut down Raimat's forces. No matter how smooth they talked, they could easily try something similar again.

Rosé, however, shook her head in denial.

"No. The mission we were given by Galerie Berith was to make you king. My Lord Yahiro Narusawa—the Dragon Slayer."

Yahiro's jaw dropped.

1

Japan had heavy precipitation all year long, which meant it was relatively blessed with bountiful water. With water and sewer services stopped after the J-nocide, though, bathing had become something of a luxury.

This meant that what moved Yahiro to his core was the shower room in the Galerie Berith armored-train facilities. Just turn the tap and hot water came out. It was like magic.

There was not much space to work with, though, so the booths themselves were cramped and the partitions thin. He could even hear the conversation going on in the women's shower room through the ceiling vents.

"Wow, Rosé, your skin's so smooth! Your waist's so thin!"

"You say that, but I must admit I envy your body, Iroha. It's impressive... exceedingly so...despicably so..."

"...Despicably?!"

Yahiro showered quietly as he listened to their candid conversation. His Lazarus body would heal only wounds that involved a certain amount of bloodshed, so the water pressure stung against his more minor injuries.

"*How were you bathing up until now?*"

"*Oh... There's a hot spring near our home, so that was no problem.*"

Rosé kept quiet for one second, suspiciously, after Iroha's answer.

"*A hot spring? Inside the 23 Wards?*"

"*Yup. Actually, we started living in there because of the spring.*"

"*I see, so this is the effect of the mystic Japanese onsen...*"

"*Uh... I–I don't think it makes them grow...*"

Iroha stammered in response to Rosé's curiously serious comment.

It certainly didn't sound like a conversation between a Moujuu tamer and the manager of arms sales. Entirely unaware of what they were even talking about, Yahiro finished showering and grabbed a towel.

Then he heard the door to the room open and someone come running in.

"Yahiro, Yahiro! How's the water? You know how to make it come out?"

"Whoa! Giuli?! What're you doing in here?!"

The booth's swinging door covered only up to Yahiro's shoulders. Giuli stood on her toes to peer above it.

"I brought you a change of clothes! And I also wanted to check out your body, so... Whoa! Impressive! Very nice!"

"Stop ogling me!"

Yahiro froze up, exposed to her lecherous gaze. He knew that, really, she was looking only at how his body had healed, but that actually made him even more self-conscious about it. And he had a towel wrapped around his hips, after all, so what was he getting so worked up about?

"I'll stop looking, so let me touch instead, okay?" And so she did, groping his arm.

"How's that any better?!"

"Oh, please, what's the harm?"

"Yahiro, what are you doing to Giuli over there?!"

"Hold on, Rosé! You can't just enter the men's bathroom like that!"

Just as he had overheard the girls' conversation, they would naturally also hear theirs. Yahiro, fed up, glanced at the ceiling as he heard Rosé's rarely emotional yelling and Iroha's shrieking.

"I'm so glad I got to shower," Iroha said cheerfully as she walked down the armored train's hallways.

She must have been worried about being all sweaty after running without rest for the whole night. She looked at her reflection in the window with absolute joy.

"I'm thankful they gave us a change of clothes, yeah," Yahiro said in a monotone.

He was feeling awkward because the conversation the girls had back there was still on his mind, and the scent of soap spread through the hallway.

Iroha paid no heed to Yahiro's feelings, however, and drew closer to him.

"Right? Although, don't you think this uniform's a bit too tight?"

"Not much worse than your streaming outfit."

"H-hey! That one's cute, though!"

Her uniform was sleeveless, exposing her shoulders and the top of her chest; it was the same one as the twins'.

They said it was that way to give them better mobility when battling, but Yahiro suspected it was more likely they were trying to use their good looks for an advantage in negotiations. A sad goal Iroha was being used for now, as well.

"Well, at least you won't get hot like that. It's summer, so that's convenient, isn't it?"

"I guess. Yeah, if you say it looks good, then it's fine."

"I never said that…"

Though astonished again by Iroha's mysteriously high self-esteem, Yahiro left it at that. It was true she looked good in it, after all.

They opened the door of the car's coupling and moved on to the next.

The following car was a freed space for dinner, with fancy furniture that contrasted sharply with the menacing armored train. The lounge was occupied by some operators playing board games, who all cheered upon seeing them enter. Yahiro was a bit confused at the enthusiastic reception.

"Yahiro! You're doing better than I expected!"

"Josh... Wei... You're all right."

"Yup. Great, isn't it? This is Yáo Guāng Xīng. It's got a forty-four-hundred-horsepower diesel-electric engine. Gets speeds of 111 kilometers per hour despite the size and weight of the armor. It even has a tilting mechanism for high speeds that's used instead for resisting the recoil of the cannons. This speed and armor is possible only thanks to the newly developed brake fluid. Only bad thing about it is the horribly hard beds." Josh proudly explained everything like a kid obsessed with trains.

"This train alone can take care of Grade-III Moujuu. It's thanks to this guy that we managed to escape the 23 Wards with those children." Yang Wei added to his explanation with a refreshing smile.

There was an unharmed rail line near Iroha's home by the Tokyo Dome ruins. They'd taken the armored train after getting surrounded by Moujuu following the failure of Operation: Kushinada Hunt and safely retreated from the 23 Wards. This must have been the ace up their sleeve Rosé had mentioned on that call.

"Right! The children! Where are they?!" Iroha jumped at Wei to ask.

Wei, though overwhelmed by her energy, nodded gladly. "They're in the car that just coupled with the train. They should be here any second."

And just as he said that, the door opened, and lots of tiny silhouettes came crashing into the lounge. Iroha's brothers and sisters.

"Mama!"

"Iroha!"

"Mamana!"

They all called her name as they ran to her.

"Everyone's here... I'm so glad you're okay!" Iroha hugged them back and started sobbing loudly.

She must have been worried this whole time, even after learning they were alive and safe.

"Um... Y-Yahiro!"

He was surprised to hear his name while watching Iroha cry. It came from a quiet-looking girl in a sailor uniform, clearly nervous.

"You're Iroha's..."

"Y-yes. I'm Ayaho Sashou! I, um, want to thank you for saving me back there!" Her voice cracked cutely as she bowed her head.

Yahiro had saved her from being attacked by a Moujuu earlier; it took him a bit to remember she was thanking him for that.

"Oh, no... I'm just glad you're okay."

He hadn't been thanked for anything in such a long time, he didn't know what to say. His awkward reply got a smile out of Ayaho, though.

Then Yahiro froze up, feeling a glare of murderous intent.

It came from Iroha. He could feel the hostility behind her eyes, telling him not to try anything with her precious sister. It also implied she would kill him if he made her cry.

What am I supposed to do, then? Yahiro pursed his lips.

A different kid peered out from behind Ayaho. The child looked like a girl at first, but they were actually a very adorable boy, around ten years of age.

"Aya, is that him? That's the guy Iroha spent the night with?" the boy said, twisting his pretty face into a naughty smile.

"Wha–?!" Ayaho gasped, red in the face.

"K-Kiri! What are you saying?!" Iroha shrieked.

Josh and the others cackled upon hearing that. Yahiro thought she should just act like it was nothing, since nothing happened, but he refrained from pointing that out, since it would likely only make things worse at this point.

"Hmm, not a bad-looking face," said the girl beside Kiri while staring at Yahiro. She looked younger than Ayaho, perhaps a fifth- or sixth-grader. She looked headstrong.

"No, Kiri, don't tease your seniors. You're being rude, too, Rinka."

A quiet-looking boy walked into their siblings' circle while staring at Yahiro. "Mama, what does it mean that you spent the night with him?"

"What?!"

Iroha's eyes wandered about as the smallest kids looked up at her with innocent curiosity. She glanced at Yahiro for help, but he pretended not to notice.

Then someone grabbed his left hand.

He looked down to find a small girl who appeared even younger than the rest. She was staring right into his eyes. Hers were mysterious, as though they were trying to absorb him.

"..."

"I-I'm sorry, Yahiro. Runa, let him go," Ayaho told her sister.

"Weird, Runa never cares for strangers," Rinka said.

"Yahiro, do you like little girls?" Kiri spouted.

Iroha's eyes widened, and her jaw dropped. "Yahiro, is that true?!"

"Why're you taking him seriously?!" he yelled at her.

It hadn't even been three minutes since the kids reunited and he already felt as exhausted as he usually did after one hour of battling Moujuu. It made him respect Iroha a bit more for putting up with them all the time.

"Iroha Mamana." Paola called her name as she entered the lounge car.

"Y-yes?!" Iroha straightened her posture upon hearing that monotonic voice.

Paola's expression was soft. There was an open ammo case by the tall girl's feet. Inside it was a white fur ball the size of a medium-size dog, staring at them. A mysterious creature that was a cross between a wolf and a bear–a Moujuu.

"Do you know this guy?"

"No...way..." Iroha fell to her knees.

The white Moujuu jumped out of the case and went to her.

"Are you...Nuemaru? *Is* it you?!" Iroha shouted, hugging the Moujuu.

It shook its fluffy tail in confirmation. Yahiro frowned at the sight of this. True enough, the white fur ball did resemble that giant Raiju.

"Nuemaru... You mean the Moujuu from back then?"

"Yes. Though...it's small now..." Paola answered Yahiro's question.

They thought the Raiju had died after RMS shot it, but it appeared that remnants of its exploded body had converged, and it survived. Moujuu sure were absurd creatures–though the Lazarus had no right to say that.

"Thank goodness... He's alive... Yahiro... Nuemaru's alive...!"

"Yes, yes, he's alive, so stop crying, okay? Hey, get off me!"

Iroha wailed as she clung to Yahiro, not giving a care that people were watching. He soon resigned himself to getting his new uniform smeared with tears and snot.

Ayaho watched the two with shock on her face. The rest of the kids observed with great curiosity, while Josh also shed some tears of sympathy for whatever reason.

It was then, in the worst moment possible, that Rosé entered the car. She stared with an appalled expression at Yahiro.

"You made her cry again?" she said.

"What d'you mean *again*?! What did *I* do?!" Yahiro protested her slander.

"Okay, relax. Let's forget about this and get something to eat.

I'm starving," Giuli said as she appeared from behind her sister and joined the chaos.

Yahiro and Iroha turned to look at each other. Besides their snack at the convenience-store ruins, he hadn't eaten anything in a whole day. He figured the same went for Iroha. Just talking about food suddenly had him famished.

"I'll explain some things to you while we eat. You're dying to know about the dragon, aren'tcha?" Giuli smiled.

They had no choice but to nod and go with it.

2

The Berith twins took Yahiro and Iroha to the observation deck—a place quite unfitting the armored train.

There was food for four already set out on the table at the center of the deck. The ingredients themselves were nothing fancy, but the dishes left both of them speechless.

"No way! Yahiro, these are…"

"Yeah… Those are Japanese dishes…"

Grilled fish, miso soup, and rolled omelet. Triangular *onigiri* wrapped in crispy seaweed. Soy-boiled kelp and pickled daikon. All served in traditional lacquered bowls.

"Our head chef, Shen, has mastered cuisine from all over the world," Giuli said with a prideful grin on her face.

"I lived in Japan before the J-nocide," said an Asian man wearing a chef's coat as he brought them cups of Japanese tea.

Most foreign nationals living in Japan had died alongside the Japanese during the J-nocide, but many of them managed to leave the country just in time. Shen must have been one of them.

"It's…delicious…," Iroha said, tears in her eyes as she nibbled her *onigiri*.

"Good to know. There's plenty more where that came from, so please eat up." The chef bowed with a pleased smile on his face.

Once he saw the man leave the room, Yahiro turned to look at the twins.

"We're receiving quite the treatment, huh?"

"It is only natural, my lord." Rosé sipped the miso soup after responding calmly.

Giuli stuffed her cheeks with *onigiri* and reached for the opposite end of the table.

"Oh, fetch me the soy sauce, my lord."

"What's this *lord* thing all about?"

You making fun of me? Yahiro frowned.

"We told you: You are the Dragon Slayer." Rosé paid no mind to the anger in Yahiro's eyes.

He pursed his lips even further, taking the comment as sarcastic.

"I haven't slain any dragons."

"That you have not. So please do so. Slay all of them." Rosé kept a straight face.

Yahiro raised an eyebrow at the casual request.

"All...of them?"

"Yes." Rosé nodded. "There was more than one dragon identified in the skies of Japan the day the J-nocide began."

"Wha...?"

"We suspect there are eight in total. Superbia—Sui Narusawa—is but one of them."

"That's...news to me..." Yahiro's voice trembled as he scowled at Rosé.

Yahiro had seen only one dragon that day: the rainbow-colored dragon Sui had summoned.

He didn't know about any others. He was totally unaware of their existence. He never once considered a dragon other than Sui's had taken part in the J-nocide.

"Naturally. It's kept highly confidential," Rosé responded, annoyed at having to explain every little thing.

"Any witnesses are dead, after all. Though there may be more exceptions like you out there." Giuli shrugged as she held the grilled fish's tail in her mouth.

Yahiro stared at them in silence.

Just recently, he had heard the same thing, actually—that there was more than one dragon. Iroha had told him so in his dream. And right after she said so, her body had been engulfed in flames, and they had healed.

"So what *are* dragons?" Iroha asked in a low voice; it sounded faint and weak, unlike her usual voice.

"That is like asking, 'What is God?'" Rosé sighed.

Iroha blinked repeatedly in confusion. "...God?"

"Long ago in ancient times, many gods and dragons were one and the same. Say, for example, gods of creation such as Quetzalcoatl and Nüwa. Or gods representing the world itself such as Ananta or Jörmungandr... Dragons create new worlds, then get slain by heroes. Such is their fate."

"They're...fated to be slain by heroes?" Iroha said fearfully, hugging herself tightly.

"Yes." Rosé nodded; then the corners of her mouth curved upward. "Which is why no dragons exist in this world anymore. Were they to appear, it would be as visitors from another world." She looked at Yahiro with a suggestive glance. "So we need someone to kill them. We will create the new hero to slay them."

"So this is why you're telling me where Sui is?" Yahiro sighed in irritation before even getting to swallow his rice ball.

It made sense to tell him about it in order to fulfill Rosé's wish to slay the dragon. And sure enough, the only shocking bit of information was that there were dragons other than Sui. It changed nothing about what he had to do.

"Wait. What is the relation between Sui and the dragon, exactly?" Iroha interrupted before Yahiro got an answer to his question.

Rosé thought for a while before deciding to give priority to Iroha's question. She grabbed her Japanese teacup with both hands and took a sip beforehand.

"Dragons need a vessel in order to manifest in this world."

"Which is...?"

"You might be familiar with the concept of sacrificial maidens."

Iroha nodded. Priestesses used to be sacrificed to the gods in more primitive times—the same idea applied for Rosé's mention of vessels.

"Say, for example, girls abducted by the evil balaur dragons. Or the nameless Libyan queen. There are many legends all over the world about maidens sacrificed to dragons," the blue-haired girl explained carefully.

Yahiro's brow furrowed slightly. He remembered Iroha being called Kushinada. The original Kushinadahime from Izumo was a girl who was supposed to be offered as a sacrifice to a dragon.

"Depending on how you see it, you could say that they summoned the dragons. The dragons appear in human form first. Iroha Mamana...that goes for you, as well." Rosé glared at her.

Iroha flinched and choked. "M-me?"

"You must've had a feeling. You think a simple human would be able to tame the Moujuu?"

"Well... Uh..." She diverted her gaze.

It was the obvious reaction. Yahiro would act the same if someone was to accuse him out of nowhere of being a dragon.

But deep inside, he knew it.

After shedding so much blood and being plunged into the death slumber, Yahiro's body had healed impossibly fast just by being near her. His second blood bath, in hers this time, had even dramatically elevated his Lazarus powers.

It all made sense if it turned out she was just like Sui.

He'd first obtained the Lazarus body after bathing in a dragon's vessel's blood—and it was enhanced on a second round.

That meant no sin on Iroha's part, however. There was no reason for her to bear any responsibility. She wasn't like Sui. Yahiro knew that.

"Our contract was only to capture Iroha, remember?" Yahiro put his palms together in gratitude for the food, then glanced at the Berith twins.

Yahiro's job was to guide them to the Kushinada's dwelling. Things had happened, and he'd had to take Iroha with him and escape the 23 Wards together, but he had fulfilled the terms of his contract.

Rosé nodded, then squinted playfully.

"I believe you don't need your reward anymore."

"Sui's captive in Raimat International, isn't she?"

"Yes. She is in the former Japan Ground Self-Defense Force's base in the Saitama prefecture—Raimat Japan's headquarters. We will get there in about two more hours."

"Wha–?! The train's heading for the Raimat base?" Yahiro opened his eyes wide.

Galerie Berith's armored train had been running without rest toward Raimat's base after exterminating RMS's main troops.

"Yes, though it's taking the scenic route. Can't go right through the 23 Wards, unfortunately." Rosé spoke casually.

"Is crushing Raimat your ultimate goal?" Yahiro glared sternly at her.

Raimat's forces were greatly decreased with their personal PMC eliminated. They could launch a surprise attack on them before they recovered, and this was a great strategy in and of itself.

The issue was, Yahiro's goal was only to kill his dragon sister, not eradicate Raimat. He did not enjoy being used to crush the twins' competitor.

Rosé shook her head, smile on her face, clearing his doubts.

"Not at all. It is not worth it."

The look of Rosé's eyes, empty like a bottomless pit, made chills run down his spine.

She wasn't lying. Raimat International was but a pebble on the side of the road to her. It needed only a kick to be thrown out of the way, nothing more.

"You wanna kill Sui, right?" Giuli asked, staring gleefully at him. "She is the dragon's vessel—its medium—and we want you to kill the dragon. It's as if we were fated to meet you."

"What a terrible fate!" Yahiro grimaced.

He tried to reflexively deny it, but it was true that their goals aligned. And he needed Galerie Berith's help to get to where Sui was being held captive.

"Shall we explain it in business terms to put you at ease?" Rosé asked calmly.

Yahiro was only confused by the proposition. "Business?"

"Yes. Galerie Berith will provide Yahiro Narusawa and Iroha Mamana all the support needed to kill the dragons. In exchange, you will kill the dragons for us. Take it as a sort of sponsorship agreement with an athlete."

"Wha...? No, no, no, what the hell?! How'd you arrive at that idea?" Iroha butted in. "Why'd you put my name in there?!"

"...Is there any issue with that?"

"Yes! There's nothing *but* issues! Yahiro, say something! Why are you all set on killing his sister in the first place?!" She scowled at him.

Yahiro looked away, out the window, then answered, "I can't let Sui go free. I'm killing her, regardless of what the twins want."

"But why?!"

"She caused the J-nocide."

"...?!" Iroha froze up.

The J-nocide was no natural disaster or accident. Sui Narusawa had wished for the massacre. She had turned Tokyo into ruins and killed all the Japanese.

"Would you forgive her even then? She could do the same thing again if we let her live."

"What…happened? Does she just…hate the whole world?" Iroha stared at him without blinking.

Yahiro did not answer the question. *If only…*, he thought.

"I will kill Sui," Yahiro said, turning to the Berith twins once again. "Iroha's got nothing to do with this. Let her be."

"Whoa! What a nice guy!" Giuli wolf-whistled mockingly like a little kid.

Iroha took it seriously and blushed.

Yahiro's face turned red as well. He glared at the orange-haired girl and said, "Shut it. I just don't want her getting in my way!"

"Oh, we would love to just let her be, but then she'd get killed. Raimat's not the only one going after dragon mediums." Giuli conveyed the heavy information with a fun smile on her face.

Iroha bit her lip. Yahiro pursed his in vexation.

"Who benefits from killing her?"

"Many past Dragon Slayers obtained the dragon's treasure for their deeds."

"…Treasure?"

They drop it like in RPGs or something? He chuckled bitterly.

Rosé tilted her head, unable to understand why he was laughing.

"Yes. The mark of a Dragon Slayer—the Regalia. For example, Sigurd's golden ring or Susanoo-no-Mikoto's Ame-no-Murakumo-no-Tsurugi."

"So is this treasure Galerie Berith's real goal?" His eyes reflected understanding immediately.

He didn't know about the golden ring, but the Ame-no-Murakumo-no-Tsurugi was one of the Three Sacred Treasures of Japan. One could easily imagine how valuable it must be. It was something a self-proclaimed galerie could never look past.

If Galerie Berith's true goal was to kill the dragon in order to obtain the Regalia, then it made perfect sense that they would help him out.

Rosé did not deny Yahiro's conjecture.

"You are free to believe so. However, it's not certain the treasure will have a physical form."

"Huh?"

Her explanation came as a surprise. He couldn't comprehend the logic behind obtaining something without physical form.

In order to clear his doubts, Rosé pointed out the window of the armored train—in the direction of the 23 Wards.

"It is believed the giant hole from which Moujuu emerge at the center of the 23 Wards was created by Sui Narusawa's Regalia—the Hollow."

"...Regalia... So that's what that meant..." Yahiro felt chills go down his spine.

All his unresolved questions surfaced like pieces of a puzzle finally nearing completion.

Why had armies from all over the world sent large troops to the deserted archipelago of Japan? Why had so many PMCs wanted to get their hands on Iroha?

Their actions were inevitable if one was to consider that a dragon's treasure could easily destroy a whole country.

It also made sense why Giuli said more people were trying to kill Iroha.

There was no way the rest of humanity would let a Japanese survivor with the dangerous powers of a dragon roam free.

They could simply capture her. If not, then at least kill her before she fell into enemy hands.

They all thought the same, which was why the Berith twins had asked him to kill *all* the dragons.

"You said there are eight dragons, right?" Yahiro asked for confirmation, his throat dry.

The girl with the orange highlights bit into a pickled plum, and her whole face puckered at the sourness.

"Yup. Though not all dragon emergences have been confirmed."

"I will only kill Sui. The others are not my problem."

"That's okay for now." Giuli smiled, tears still in her eyes. "We've got a deal, then. Pinkie swear?"

"...Why?" Yahiro was taken aback by Giuli reaching out her right pinkie finger.

"Huh?" Giuli tilted her head. "Isn't this Japanese tradition?"

"I mean... I guess...? In a way?" Yahiro was overwhelmed by her enthusiasm and entwined his pinkie finger with hers.

Iroha observed with mixed feelings rising to her face.

"What about you, Iroha Mamana?" Rosé asked.

Iroha's big eyes wavered for a moment before she nodded with determination and verbally agreed to the contract with the girls like she was signing away her soul to the devil.

3

"What do you mean, you can't help?"

Count Hector Raimat yelled at the low-resolution screen in the Raimat branch headquarters command room.

The man on the other side of the line was the branch manager of big-name military company D9S. The count had just begun negotiating with this colleague to get D9S to lend him operators from their PMC division.

"It's just as I said, Count. My troops were sent to Sendai city to exterminate Moujuu; unfortunately, we do not have enough forces to lend you for protection. If you could only wait two weeks, then we could call for extra operators from our homeland," the branch manager explained pragmatically.

He spoke cordially, but it was obvious he did not want to deal with this. He only wanted to turn down the count politely.

"Raimat will pay the sum for the breach of contract. Please, could you just send the troops deployed to Sendai over here right away?" the count continued, holding down his anger.

D9S was an international conglomerate of nine military

companies. Their PMC division had an exceedingly high number of human resources, reaching levels tantamount to a superpower's military.

On the financial side, Raimat International wasn't too far behind them, but the scope of the corporation bore no significance in the current situation.

RMS's main troop, deployed to the 23 Wards, had been exterminated. By Galerie Berith. Raimat's Japanese branch's forces were now at the lowest they had ever been.

Raimat wouldn't be able to withstand a surprise attack from any other PMC now. They needed to replenish their forces before that happened. Securing operators was their utmost priority.

He had called D9S because he was counting on their abundant resources, but...

"That I cannot allow, Count. The Canadian Army controlling the Miyagi area is one of our best customers. We cannot allow ourselves to lose their trust now." The branch manager immediately dismissed the idea.

His argument, on the surface, was ironclad; the count had nothing to say to that.

The branch manager smiled smugly and added, *"First of all, Raimat International has its own PMC division to take care of itself. RMS, was it? Why couldn't you call them back from the 23 Wards? If there are any forces left to call back, that is..."*

"Son of a...!" The veins on the count's head bulged.

D9S knew RMS's main troop had been wiped out. And they knowingly turned down the count's call for help. They had clearly abandoned Raimat, siding with Galerie Berith instead.

"Well then, Count. I must go. Send my regards to the Berith twins." The D9S branch manager cut off the transmission with those audacious parting words.

The count, humiliated, couldn't speak for a few moments.

"Galerie Berith... You're well prepared, I see!" The count gripped his cane hard, finally understanding the extent of the situation.

Ranga Patna, Queensland Defense Service, D9S...all PMCs in the Kanto area had refused to help the count. Galerie Berith had contacted them beforehand in order to isolate Raimat.

He had planned to use them all as bait to safely capture the Kushinada, but out of the blue, the tables had turned. He couldn't contain his anger.

"What about RMS's reinforcement troops?"

"We asked the homeland to send two battalions, but it is taking them time to secure personnel and transport. It might take them four days at the very least..."

"So we have to make do with what we have here until then... La Hire...that incompetent bastard!" The count clicked his tongue after hearing his secretary's report.

It was all thanks to Firman La Hire falling into the Beriths' trap. They had lost all the Fafnir soldiers entrusted to him, and he had even let the Kushinada escape.

Galerie Berith's forces were not that big when compared to other PMCs. Calling them an *"elite few"* made it sound good, but in truth, they were barely offsetting their lack of men with the quality of their operators.

Yet now, Raimat had no way to fight against such a small force. The RMS headquarters were all the way back in Europe—getting reinforcements in half a day was physically impossible.

Meanwhile, Galerie Berith was acting fast. He could guess they would be raiding the base in less than two hours.

And they had the Lazarus to boot. Not even the Fafnir soldiers would be able to stop Galerie Berith's invasion so long as they had that irritating Japanese boy on their side.

The count was beginning to seriously consider abandoning the base and running for it.

Losing the facilities would be a great loss, but not something they wouldn't be able to recuperate in time. They would have their chance to strike back against Galerie Berith eventually.

The most important thing to take was the data on the Fafnir soldiers' application and the main source of material for the F-med—the dragon medium. So long as he had that in his hands, money would take care of anything else.

Ganzheit wouldn't allow him to transport the dragon medium of his own accord, naturally, but were they to get in his way, worst-case scenario, he could kill their auditor, Auguste Nathan...

His hostile train of thought was cut short by someone speaking.

"You appear troubled, Count."

"...?!" He turned around fearfully.

A tall Black man wearing a fancy suit was standing beside him suddenly. Auguste Nathan, surprisingly outside of his lab.

"Sir Nathan? What's the matter? You don't have clearance to be here..."

"I heard Major La Hire's Fafnir-soldier troop was wiped out. The fire dragon, Avaritia, awakened and granted the Beriths' Lazarus with the Blaze Regalia?" Nathan ignored the count's accusation.

The aura Nathan's tall body exuded was intimidating.

"Why...do you know all this?"

"The Fafnir soldiers are her familiars. It shouldn't be strange that she would feel their absence," Nathan replied with disinterest, like it was nothing.

In contrast, the count shuddered upon hearing that. Even more so when he saw the girl appear behind Nathan.

Her hair was white, as though lacking any pigment. She was almost fifteen, but she looked much younger. Her limbs were devoid of muscle after the long years she'd spent slumbering. This, added to the luxurious gothic dress like a western doll's, made her look like a beautiful ghost roaming a desolate old castle.

"Brynhildr... You're awake, Sui Narusawa?!" The count stared at the girl in terror.

Sui's large eyes coldly took in her surroundings.

The staff in the command room knew nothing of Sui Narusawa's identity, but they each understood instinctively that she was an odd being. They all winced, holding their breath like helpless prey before a giant predator.

"You're in need of troops, are you not? Then thank her. She will assist you." Nathan spoke with a dignified tone.

The earth shook immediately after.

The air itself creaked as a storm raged. All windows in the room shattered, and outside, they could see pitch-black holes absorbing the light around them.

"The Hollow...Regalia...!" the count exclaimed hoarsely.

The Raimat base was filled with pits about forty feet in diameter. They were full of darkness, nothing more to see. Not until something began crawling out of them. Monsters that ignored the taxonomy of normal creatures. Moujuu.

"You intend to turn the base into a Moujuu nest, Auguste Nathan?!" the count yelled in anger, now beyond fear.

The Moujuu would surely get in Galerie Berith's way, but they wouldn't only attack the invaders. The first ones to become their prey would be the count's underlings, in fact.

"Stop shouting, Count. Show some respect and composure before the dragon," Nathan said haughtily before handing him something.

It was a cylinder filled with a fluid similar to the F-med. This was not crimson in color, however—it was nearly colorless.

"What is this?"

"It's what you wanted. Not a fake like the F-med. Real dragon blood."

The count's jaw dropped, and his hand holding the container trembled. The emotion behind his eyes was that of joy.

"The Ichor for immortality... With this, can I become a Lazarus, too?"

"If you have what it takes."

The white-haired girl beside Nathan smiled after his curt response. It was a beautiful yet cruel, frosty smile.

She turned and left, the tall Black man following behind her like her loyal knight.

Before leaving the room, Nathan turned back to the count and, with a flat tone, warned him:

"Make haste with your choice, Count. You're out of time."

4

It was Josh who first noticed the shift, as he was looking out the armored train's hatch.

Raimat's Japanese branch, built upon the remains of the JSDF base, was engulfed in smoke. The giant facility was burning despite its robust defense systems.

"What in the world?!" Josh exclaimed as he looked through the binoculars.

The cause of the fire was clear as day even from afar: Moujuu. Dozens of spectral beasts had emerged in its grounds and were now destroying everything in their path.

"That's Raimat's Japanese branch?! How'd it get infested with Moujuu?!"

"Amazing. It's 23 Wards–tier... No, it's even worse." Yang Wei's expression turned grave as he watched the live drone feed.

Yahiro agreed in silence. He was used to going through the 23 Wards, and he had never seen so many Moujuu gathered in one place. It felt like looking directly into the supposed source of the beasts—the Ploutonion.

"That is the earth dragon's, Superbia's, Hollow Regalia... It seems Sui Narusawa is awake," Rosé stated with her usual monotone, now wearing her uniform and fully armed.

"Sui...did this?" Yahiro was taken aback by the blue-haired girl's words.

It wouldn't be unlike her to unleash Moujuu right where she

was if she knew Yahiro was coming for her. It was her own way of greeting him.

"Giuli, Rosé… What should we do about the survivors?" Paola asked flatly.

Many Raimat employees had already died at the hands of the Moujuu, but there were still quite a few others running away from the beasts. She was asking the bosses whether to save them or let them die.

"Your team can let anyone who surrenders into the Yáo Guāng Xīng. Don't forget to disarm them. Wei, your team will be guarding the train. Don't let any Moujuu near the tracks."

"Got it…"

"Roger, Giuli."

"Life is sacred, right?" Giuli smiled.

Paola and Wei nodded simultaneously.

The railway was just over 457 meters away from the Raimat base. The Moujuu would rush over to the Yáo Guāng Xīng the moment the battle began. Having to spare a team to guard the train was unexpected but the best course of action.

"Which means we'll be going with the ladies." Josh grinned at Yahiro while holding up his precious machine gun.

The team leaders needn't hear any announcement to know the Berith twins would be leading and charging into the Raimat base. Yahiro wasn't happy about being treated as their attendant, though. *Where did I go wrong with my choices?*

"What about you, Iroha?" Rosé asked her, ignoring Yahiro's discontent.

"This…is the power of a dragon? Sui really did this?" she muttered, staring at the live drone feed.

Structures collapsing. People fleeing. The Moujuu wreaked havoc as soon as they emerged, attacking even their own kind. It was hell on earth. And if the twins were right, it was what Sui Narusawa wished for.

"I'll go, too," she stated firmly, finally deciding to cooperate with Galerie Berith.

"Iroha," Yahiro interjected.

There was a war going on outside the train. Dragon medium or not, she had lived entirely detached from war among humans; it wasn't a sight she had to behold.

"I can get the Moujuu to stop attacking people!" Iroha said to his face.

Yahiro could not argue back.

He had seen her tame the beasts countless times during their trek across the uncharted lands. If her power worked even here, then she could neutralize a good portion of the raging Moujuu at least. And Galerie Berith didn't have enough forces to just let those neutralized Moujuu roam free.

"Giuli and I will guard her. Is that all right, Yahiro?"

"Do as you please." Yahiro shrugged in response to Rosé's question, capitulating.

The railway screeched as the armored train came to a stop. The freight car for vehicle transport was disconnected, and two armored vehicles landed on the ground right away.

Yahiro opened the troop carrier's door and jumped out of the vehicle. The smoking Raimat base was before him.

5

"Stop. Don't. Don't go there," Iroha reached out both hands, unarmed, and called to the Moujuu.

It was a big one, unnamed. It looked like a crocodile mixed with a borzoi hound. Likely Grade II. Iroha looked dreadfully small beside its buffalo-size body, and yet, the vicious beast kneeled at her glance.

"Don't attack any human. Stay here and protect the train."

The Moujuu turned around, having understood Iroha's orders. It drove away the other nearby beasts.

"That's amazing, Iroha. Guess the Kushinada name wasn't for show." Josh put his gun down and ran up to her, exhaling in admiration.

Josh had seen Iroha mount the white Raiju back at her home, but it was the first time he saw her tame a wild Moujuu. He felt no fear about it, however, instead only applauding her like a hyped kid.

"Um, yeah, I suppose." Iroha nodded and wiped sweat from her cheek. "But I'm a little scared of these guys. I have to get really close for them to hear me. They're so terrified and angry, the poor guys."

"It must be because they're under the control of another dragon on your same level," Rosé explained.

Iroha gasped.

Sui had summoned the Moujuu in the base through the Plouton-ion. Even if they had no direct orders from her, they were naturally affected by her will. The anger and fear Iroha felt from them were in part directed toward Sui.

"But hey, at least we can keep moving without getting interrupted by the Moujuu. Thanks!" Giuli hugged Iroha with a sincere smile on her face.

"True," Josh said, and his subordinates nodded in agreement.

The Galerie's operators were unharmed so far thanks to Iroha taming all Moujuu they encountered.

Meanwhile, Raimat's guards were nearly annihilated after the beasts emerged inside the base. Yahiro and the rest were able to reach the main building without fighting them.

"Giuli, capture a couple of Raimat officers—alive."

"We're interrogating them, eh? Cool, I'll do it."

The elder twin agreed without hesitation and kicked down the glass door to enter the base's lobby.

The security systems were still up: a sentry gun reacted

immediately, but before it could shoot Giuli, Rosé destroyed it with her own assault rifle.

Meanwhile, Giuli neutralized all guards in the room. They had held up against the Moujuu but were powerless against the nimble, unarmed girl.

"Josh's team will split in two to keep an eye on the surroundings. Yahiro...," Rosé whispered while deftly changing her rifle's magazine, "...you take care of Iroha."

"What?" Yahiro glanced at Iroha in confusion and immediately understood why Rosé had said that.

Iroha looked fatigued. Her expression was stiff and her breath short. She had been thrown into the middle of a battlefield and made to tame multiple Moujuu; weariness wasn't surprising, but she looked even more worn out than she should've been.

It likely had to do with Sui. This was her territory; Iroha was an outsider. Perhaps her dragon instincts were instilling the fear of another dragon's presence in her.

"She's in your hands. I'll be looking for Sui Narusawa's location."

"Hey, Rosé—!"

She entered the building without hearing Yahiro out. Her plan was to get intel from the captured guards. She left Iroha outside so as to not let her see the interrogation and did the same for Yahiro by making him look out for her.

Yahiro understood Rosé did it from consideration for them, but he wasn't entirely happy about it. He didn't know what to do now.

"Um... You okay, Iroha?"

Iroha was leaning back against their vehicle when Yahiro awkwardly called out to her. She raised her head in slight surprise, then forced a smile.

"Thanks, Yahiro. I'm okay. Mind if I lean on you for a bit?" she asked right as she rested her head on his shoulder.

Their skin touched, and Yahiro noticed she was abnormally hot. Then he understood why she was so tired. Both he and Rosé had it wrong. Iroha wasn't afraid—quite the opposite. There was this fierce power swirling inside her, itching for the moment to break out. She was holding it in with her all, using her whole energy to not let the dragon out.

Then, perhaps as a result of coming in close contact with Yahiro, all tension left her shoulders. And so they got a moment to cuddle, right in the middle of the battlefield.

"I had this dream," Iroha muttered, eyes still closed.

"What was it?"

"I dreamed of this other world, far away from here. A world in ruins. Memories of myself before I became me."

"…" He silently urged her to go on. He felt there had to be a meaning to her suddenly remembering this dream right in this moment.

"I was the last one in that world. I had no choice but to perish alongside it, but then a dragon appeared before my eyes… No, I mean, that dragon is myself… Um, I'm having a hard time explaining it, sorry."

"That's just how dreams work."

"Ah-ha-ha… You're right…" Iroha smiled weakly at Yahiro's awkward reassurance. "Anyway, in this dream, I met a dragon. A dragon other than me. I met eight dragons, actually."

Yahiro then remembered she had once told him she met Sui in a dream.

"I don't know why, but I knew right away, when I met them, that all of them were the last survivors of their own worlds."

Yahiro felt her body curl up in fear.

The last survivors of dead worlds. Crushing, eternal loneliness. He immediately knew she feared this to her core.

"Rosé said dragons create new worlds…and that's when I remembered. That maybe we were given another chance. A chance to rebuild our lost worlds from zero…"

Her whispering monologue suddenly changed to feeble screams.

"But there's only one world here and eight dragons…which means we're all in one another's way. So long as others with the same power exist, our wish to build our own world will never come true!"

"So the dragons must kill one another because of that?"

"I suppose…" Iroha embraced Yahiro's shoulder with trembling arms. She caught her breath before continuing. "But I can't accept that. I don't want to let the dragons destroy this world to rebuild it as they wish…"

"I see…" Yahiro gently placed his hand on Iroha's head, like he once had, so long ago he couldn't remember anymore, to his own sister. "Then don't."

"What?" Iroha was taken aback by Yahiro's irresponsible answer.

He paid it no mind and continued. "It's just a dream, right? I think you should do whatever you want."

"I mean, maybe so, but…"

"And if the other dragons get in your way, I'll protect you. I'll be by your side," Yahiro said bluntly while looking away from Iroha's point-blank stare.

He saw Iroha's eyes widen out of the corner of his eye.

"Yahiro…!"

"But that'll only be…"

"After we stop Sui, right? I know. We can't let her do this!" Iroha bit her lip as she looked slowly all around.

The fight in the base was reaching its end. Some of Raimat's employees ran away from the premises, while the rest were devoured by the Moujuu. Many of the beasts had fallen, too, at the hands of the guards' relentless resistance and the armored train's bombardment. The perimeter was lined with mountains of corpses and reeked of blood.

And it was Sui's malice that had created this scene.

Plus, Iroha was feeling guilty about it, for not stopping her fellow dragon medium.

"Iroha."

"Huh...?"

Yahiro violently pushed her shoulder. She was entirely leaning on him, so it made her lose her balance and fall. She glared up at him, frowning, but then she froze.

Something had broken a window on the base's third floor and fallen down. It landed gracefully from more than nine meters high. Its silhouette was crimson, scaly, human with dragon traits.

"A Fafnir soldier?!"

"Kept us waiting..."

Iroha's jaw dropped in fear, while Yahiro unsheathed the katana from his back.

6

The dragonman extended his vicious claws, howling as he glared at Iroha.

New Fafnir soldiers appeared one after the other.

The torn clothes barely clinging to their bodies were not operator uniforms but suits and dress shirts belonging to white-collar workers. Raimat had used the F-med on regular employees to stand against the Moujuu emergence.

There was fire in their eyes—no trace of human intellect remained. The F-med had made the men—unused to battle—lose their minds.

"Hide, Iroha!" Yahiro gripped his sword tight.

He had remade Kuyo Masakane's *koshirae* sword sling, broken in the battle against RMS, with the 3-D printer in the armored train. Unfortunately, this gave it a look too modern for a legendary katana, but Yahiro didn't care so long as it could cut down his enemies.

"...They're fast?!" Yahiro frowned at the agility with which the Fafnir soldiers assaulted.

They were abnormally quick, even when compared to Firman's

Mod-3. Not that he had any way to measure it, but it also felt like their strength was further amplified, too. This wasn't because the F-med had been upgraded, though.

One of the soldiers punched the armored carrier and put a huge dent in armor capable of resisting antimaterial rifle shots. However, the recoil absolutely crushed the soldier's right arm. The soldiers' limbs couldn't withstand their movements; their arms and legs were in a continuous cycle of death and rebirth.

"Was this Sui, too?!" Yahiro gritted his teeth upon realizing the source behind the Fafnir soldiers' state.

The F-med's source material being Sui's blood, it was entirely natural for the soldiers to be under her influence. Sui's aura filling the surroundings of the base affected them just as it did the summoned Moujuu, increasing their hostility.

"...Tsk!" Yahiro, burning with ire, slashed the Fafnir soldiers' legs.

The enhanced soldiers didn't have upgraded regenerative abilities. A deep cut all the way to the bone was still enough to stop them. But this also meant there were no other ways to neutralize them without killing them. And having to fight while missing the opponents' vitals only drew him further and further into a corner among the swarm of Fafnir soldiers.

Should I use the Lazarus blood to kill them? The idea crossed his mind for a moment, but he immediately shook it off.

These weren't combatants. They were not like the men who had attacked them back in the 23 Wards. He realized right away that this was what Sui wanted—to have Yahiro kill the berserkers with his own hands.

"Yahiro, pull back!"

He trusted Giuli's voice and jumped back and away from the melee.

A silver glow spread like sheer silk right before his eyes. A spiderweb. A fine steel-wire casting net. Giuli had shot it, compressed into the size of a hand grenade, before it unraveled to shroud the Fafnir soldiers.

"It's a prototype, developed for capturing Moujuu, but I suppose it works on them, too." Rosé spoke emotionlessly, coming back out from the building.

The Fafnir soldiers' strength wasn't enough to tear the anti-Moujuu wire. The more they struggled, the further entangled they became.

The net had missed a few of them, but the Galerie's operators neutralized them by shooting their legs. They had also dealt with a group that appeared inside the building in the same way.

"Is the interrogation over?" Yahiro asked Rosé while lowering his sword.

"No, there's no longer any need for interrogations." Rosé slowly glanced around.

There was a man Yahiro didn't recognize standing beyond the Fafnir soldiers trapped in the net. A tall Black man wearing a fancy suit. His visage was quiet and intellectual, but there was an intensely imposing air about him that had Yahiro unconsciously on guard. He felt shivers go down his spine in a way he had never felt before.

"I suppose this is as far as hastily made Fafnir soldiers can go. How regrettable. I was hoping for them to make Yahiro Narusawa unleash his Regalia." The man spoke in a calm yet oddly loud and clear voice.

Galerie Berith's operators all pointed their guns at him in sync, but the man paid them no mind as he stared only at Yahiro and Iroha.

"Ohgusu Neisan… What's a Ganzheit agent doing here?" Giuli asked the man in a rare display of irritation.

Yahiro felt that something was off about the man's name—the way Giuli had pronounced it.

"Neisan?"

"You see, my parents naturalized before I was born. As surprising as it may sound, I am Japanese through and through. Or, well, I would be if Japan still existed." Neisan was surprisingly frank in clearing his doubts.

Yahiro was aghast.

It wouldn't have been hard to conceal his nationality, considering his looks, but the man showed no hesitation in declaring himself Japanese even after the J-nocide. Yahiro felt respect for that attitude, yet he couldn't shake the feeling that there could be something behind his doing so.

"Since when did Ganzheit begin taking sides?" Rosé criticized Neisan harshly. More than personally offended, she sounded like a referee calling out some cheating.

"Ganzheit has never shown you antagonism. It was not our will to use Raimat but hers." Neisan glanced to his side.

It was then that they noticed the presence of that girl.

She wore a luxurious gothic dress, entirely out of place on this bloody battlefield. Her hair and skin were white, like they were devoid of all pigment. Only her lips remained colored, in vivid crimson. Her limbs were sickly thin, making her look like a fantastical being, like a fairy. Her big eyes, decorated by long eyelashes, looked like still water, lacking emotion.

"Mr. Ohgusu was merely going along with my whims. I wanted to greet you all." The girl curtsied gracefully.

Yahiro scowled at her, the katana in his hand trembling.

"Su…i…!" Anger rumbled from his throat like a beast's roar.

The girl glanced at him and narrowed her eyes in amusement.

"Good evening, Dear Brother. I am glad to see you alive." Sui Narusawa giggled with a beautiful voice, like a bell's gentle chime. Her smile was sweet enough to melt whoever gazed upon it. "Could it be you were simply unable to die this whole time? Just like four years ago—"

"*Suiii!*"

It was then that his murderous rage exceeded its limits. He kicked the ground with boiling rage and slashed the dully shining katana upward.

A cracked crimson armor enveloped Yahiro's body in reaction to his rampaging emotions, as though the dragon blood had seeped out to the surface of his body.

Yahiro's physical abilities skyrocketed in sync with his armor's emergence. All latent human power rose to the surface, ignoring any possible damage to his body. Even Josh and the other veteran operators were stunned by his transformation.

Sui, meanwhile, locked eyes with Yahiro's homicidal stare and smiled even more graciously.

Neisan took a step forward, hiding Sui behind him. Yahiro grimaced the moment he saw the tall man's left arm—covered in crystalized metal luster just like his own body.

"What?!"

Neisan stopped Yahiro's katana with his bare hand.

A thick, invisible shield appeared before him. Yahiro was blown backward in the recoil of his own attack.

"That's it for the Blaze? No, I doubt you've mastered your Regalia," Neisan muttered flatly, staring blankly at Yahiro's faltering landing. His tone was that of an observer monitoring a rare physical phenomenon.

"That arm... You're...," Yahiro mumbled as he glared at Neisan's left arm, covered in Goreclad the color of Sui's hair.

"Presumptuous of you to assume you are the only Lazarus, don't you think, Yahiro Narusawa?"

Yahiro tried attacking again, but he hit Neisan's invisible shield.

Yahiro's armor broke, fresh blood gushing out. He fell to the ground, defenseless.

Yet Neisan did not attempt to counter. His only objective was to guard Sui. He was telling the truth when he said he had no intention of antagonizing them.

They weren't about to accept that, though.

"Josh!"

"On it!" he answered to Giuli's sharp call.

The Galerie Berith operators pulled their triggers. High-caliber anti-Moujuu bullets rained full-auto on Sui, but again, Neisan's invisible wall stopped all of them.

"What's that? What's going on, Lady? Think a grenade could take care of that?"

"No, Josh. Not even a tank could break that. That's the power to close the Ploutonion—Chibiki-no-Iwa. It's one of the Hollow Regalia's applications." Rosé answered Josh's question.

"Wha...? So that's a Regalia?! It's even crazier than the rumors!" Josh shrugged in resignation, having emptied his light machine gun's magazine.

According to Japanese mythology, the god Izanagi blocked the way to the underworld through the Yomotsu Hirasaka slope using the Chibiki-no-Iwa—"the rock pulled by a thousand." Neisan's barrier of the same name isolated Sui from the outside world.

Yahiro couldn't kill her despite being right in front of her; the fact filled him with blinding rage and desperation.

Sui pointed her slender finger at the ground, as though mocking him. Then the earth quaked.

The ground at their feet swayed like a summer haze, transforming.

It was a giant pit. A pit filled with black water that reflected no light.

More precisely, it was closer to the miasma flowing inside the Moujuu's body. A substance that didn't exist in this world. A materialized void.

They hurriedly jumped away from the pit—the newly made Ploutonion.

The Fafnir soldiers trapped in the net screamed as the pit swallowed them. And in their place, two Moujuu emerged from the surface of the blackness: a two-meter tall, two-headed hound and a buffalo with the body of a pterosaur.

"Yahiro! Take care of Iroha!" Giuli shouted at him before running toward the Moujuu.

The tips of her gloves shot a silver wire. It flew with the wind and moved all according to Giuli's movements like a rhythmic gymnast's, binding the ox-headed pterosaur.

Meanwhile, Rosé had changed weapons to the antimaterial rifle on the armored carrier. She hugged the sniper rifle, as big as her own body, as she lay on her belly on the ground, precisely aiming at the bound Moujuu's forehead and shooting.

"Gwoooh!"

Josh and his underlings concentrated fire on the two-headed dog while the twins took care of the other. They reacted perfectly against the Moujuu's sudden emergence.

Yet the Moujuu-spitting pit did not end there. It pushed a few more beasts to the surface before the first two were completely defeated.

The objective of Sui's summoned beasts was Iroha, standing back, defenseless.

"Iroha...!" Yahiro regretfully ground his teeth as he turned his back on Neisan. He gave up on attacking Sui, instead running desperately to protect Iroha.

Sui's eyes darkened in disappointment as she saw him go, but the following moment, she was raising her eyebrows. The Moujuu about to attack Iroha came to a sudden halt, kneeling.

"Stop this, Sui!" Iroha walked toward her as the Moujuu followed like loyal retainers. "Why are you doing this?! Why did you summon the Moujuu?! Why destroy the world?!"

Sui stared back at her in silence. Her expression was not that of interest; she looked as though she was gazing upon a rare bug.

Then she clasped her hands together before her chest and giggled.

"Oh... I remember now where I've seen you. You're that streamer. What was it, again? Wown?"

"You know about Waon?" Iroha looked surprised. She wasn't

expecting to converse about her streams in the middle of a bullet rain.

Sui smiled even further in amusement at the reaction.

"Let me answer your question. I believe you would understand. Have you ever gotten mean comments on your stupid videos?"

"Huh...?" Iroha froze up, bewildered by the question.

Sui smiled innocently like a saint as she continued:

"Isn't it fun trampling on things others hold dear? They think they're all so safe, but then you hit them with the nastiness, just absolutely ruin their day. Let me show you: Freedom, love, goodwill—they're utterly useless."

The white-haired girl in the gothic dress narrowed her eyes ecstatically.

"What...are you saying...?" Iroha stared at her, aghast.

Stop it, Yahiro screamed internally. He couldn't allow their conversation to go on any further; he couldn't let Iroha hear Sui out.

And yet, his voice wouldn't come.

Neisan's hostile aura was binding. He couldn't take his focus off his own back, or the man would attack immediately.

Letting Sui act freely was his aim—having the two mediums converse was his wish.

"Who helped the Japanese during the J-nocide? How many people spoke up against their leaders?" Sui questioned Iroha back. "None. They all thought they were in the right! They all scorned the Japanese, they harmed us, they destroyed, destroyed, destroyed everything until there was no turning back!"

"Did you...cause the J-nocide just for that? Just to prove they would do that...?" Iroha stared at Sui, face pale.

The Moujuu Sui summoned were instilled with enmity toward humans. What if she could have the same effect on people? What if any human who witnessed the dragon was instilled with hatred toward the Japanese?

The answer lay in the J-nocide.

A single girl's malice had annihilated a whole country's people.

"What sort of excuses would they spout once they realized they were in the wrong? Would they repent the fact that they got carried away in support of the massacre? Would they self-reflect? Would they hide the fact and pretend nothing had happened? Would they get angry, instead, lash out at the accuser? We can't have that. We can't allow it. Not us poor, poor victims."

Sui laughed out loud; her laughing voice was lovely, not a shred of madness in it. Which made it all the eerier.

"It is time for revenge. It is time to show the people of the world true fear—show them what genocide feels like."

"I'm not letting you do that!" Iroha's yell interrupted Sui's laughter.

Yahiro's view was tinted by a bluish-white flash the next moment.

A hot gust hit his face. Scorching fire was whirling around Iroha and bursting from the earth's core like magma.

The fire converged in multiple flame pillars, rising high above the roof of the Raimat base. Then they took the form of scorching flashes of light and rained down on the ground.

The fire torrents aimed for Sui's pits. The pitch-black water burned up instantaneously, wiping out the voids.

Yahiro stared flabbergasted while Giuli and Rosé cracked a smile.

Neisan's facial expression remained the same, but his eyes looked strangely pleased.

"You purified my Hollow...?" Sui blinked in shock.

Iroha's flames were still burning on the ground, but Sui's voids had vanished. Her cataclysms overwritten.

"I see... So this is the power of the fire Regalia... Heh. You are quite fascinating." Sui smiled, staring at Iroha, who was on the ground and out of energy. It was a more becoming smile of a girl her age, unlike the empty one she had shown up to then. Like a child who had just found a new playmate.

Yahiro tensed his body as he noticed an aberrant aura enveloping Sui's surroundings.

She softly stretched her left hand out, ready to bring about a new cataclysm, but then Neisan calmly grabbed her arm.

"It is time, Sui."

"...It's here already?" She pursed her lips into a pout.

Neisan nodded in silence, then glanced upward.

"This sound! A chopper's coming!" Josh looked up in shock upon hearing the noise.

An ashen military helicopter descended before them. Yahiro figured out Neisan had called it so Sui could escape.

"Yáo Guāng Xīng! Shoot it down!" Giuli shouted into the radio.

The chopper was barely eight hundred meters away from the armored train. Easily within shooting range. However, the shells bounced off an invisible wall right before they could touch it.

"This is what the Regalia is all about, Yahiro Narusawa. To kill dragons and steal their powers, uncontrollable by regular humans—that is the role of the Lazarus. Keep it in mind," Neisan stated.

The military chopper, protected by the invisible barrier, openly descended until just a few inches above the ground. The armored train stopped shooting out of fear of hitting allies instead. All of Rosé's shots, aimed at Sui instead of the chopper, were stopped by Neisan's wall as well.

Neisan easily carried Sui up with his right arm and put a foot on the chopper's boarding step.

"Sui!" Yahiro glared at his sister, sword in hand.

He focused his mind on that feeling he'd had when he defeated Firman.

Iroha's flames had purified Sui's Ploutonions. He only had to do the same. He just had to offset Neisan's Regalia with his own.

And yet, despite being acutely aware of this, he couldn't move. It wasn't like the fight against RMS, when only thoughts of protecting

Iroha had filled his mind. He didn't even know how to activate his Regalia.

"Give up, Dear Brother. Insist too much and your precious friends will pay the price." Sui smiled from the helicopter, seeing right through his desperation.

Her words were much too clear to Yahiro's ears even among the noise of the helicopter.

Sui took her eyes off restless Yahiro with satisfaction and turned them over to Iroha.

"Don't let any other dragon kill you before we meet again, okay, little Waon? Ciao."

The helicopter rose quickly into the air with both aboard.

Yahiro could only despise the bitter taste of defeat as the transport flew away.

The sister he had sought for four long years had been right within his reach, and yet, he was incapable of killing her. He'd let her go, and now she would go on to kill even more people. Just like she'd massacred the Japanese branch of Raimat where she was supposedly being held captive.

Yahiro slowly put down his sword, powerless, disoriented.

Then he heard two sounds echo behind him: Giuli's scream and a gunshot.

7

"Your precious friends will pay the price."

Sui's parting words immediately came to mind.

Yahiro turned desperately and had no words for what he saw there.

Chaos overflowed from the Raimat base lobby.

Not Moujuu. Not even Fafnir soldiers. Carrion. A whole pool's worth of moving, putrid flesh. No other way to describe this monster.

"God, that's gross! Josh, do something about it!"

"It's useless, Princess! The guns aren't working on it!"

Josh and his team clung in tears to Giuli as they ran away while firing their machine guns.

The giant carrion that came crawling from inside the building wasn't in the least affected by the bullets. It wasn't even clear whether they caused it pain at all. Then a tentacle came out of the monster, grabbing Josh's leg like a whip.

"Gwoh?!" He fell down, pulled by its tremendous strength.

He immediately tried shooting back, but the carrion did not stop.

"Josh!" Yahiro jumped in front of the carrion and sliced the tentacle in two.

Josh, freed right before being absorbed into the lump of dead meat, shrieked as he fell back to the ground.

"I owe you one, man." He frowned as he kicked away what remained of the tentacle wrapped around his leg.

Yahiro cut off the tentacle, still reaching out for them, then retreated with Josh.

"What the hell is this?"

"Hell if I know. It just popped out of the building and swallowed a bunch of Raimat guys."

"It...swallowed them?" Yahiro asked back, shivering.

Soon the monster escaped the lobby completely, showing its full, hideous body.

Incredibly, the lump of flesh had human shape. The fat, smooth monster crawling on the ground was more than nine meters long.

On the monster's surface were traces of various living creatures. Four mammal limbs. Bat wings. A human head with empty eyes. They all wriggled in a disorderly way, buried in the lumps of flesh. The sight of it alone defiled the form of any and all living creatures.

"It's got Moujuu inside...," Iroha, still on the ground, muttered in a trembling voice.

The monster was slowly heading toward Iroha. It wasn't so much doing it out of instinct but rather willful intention—it showed in its movements. The creature wanted Iroha in its hands even now, even when degraded into a heap of rotten meat.

"Did Sui do that, too?" Yahiro asked the sisters as they came back to protect Iroha.

Giuli grimaced and shook her head. "No, that's a human. A failed Lazarus."

"...Human? That thing?"

"I suppose not anymore, but he was. Turned into this after trying to obtain an immortal body, bathing in dragon Ichor. Isn't that right, Count?" Rosé addressed the carrion.

The monster's giant head surfaced in response. Yahiro immediately felt the urge to throw up. He recognized the face that emerged from within the putrid flesh.

"Nooo, Signorinaaa Berüüth! Aaand ciaooo, Galerieee Berüüth fellooows!" the monster thundered in the count's voice.

Chairman of Raimat International Hector Raimat himself was the carrion monster, the core of the rotten flesh that kept on growing.

"You call this...a Lazarus...?" Rage boiled within Yahiro.

It was not much different from the Fafnir soldiers going berserk after overdosing on F-med, but the key point was that the dragon Ichor the count had used was far more powerful. Powerful enough to keep him alive as his body kept on growing.

This also meant that Yahiro's blood would not be able to defeat him. Moujuu and Fafnir soldiers perished in reaction to dragon blood, but the count's body was already in a state of constant perishing. He already bathed in even purer dragon blood—Yahiro's wouldn't have any effect. The count was technically a Lazarus just on the basis of his retaining human form.

"Yes! Yes! YEEES! It feels so rüüght... Finally, I've achieved iüt... I've achieved immortalityyy!" The lump of what used to be the count shook its whole body joyfully. *"Looooh! Look at all this poweeer! Not even the*

Moujuu will stand against meee! No need to fear agüing or sickneeess! I've got all the power in my haaands! Unlimited poweeer!"

A tentacle sprouted from the count's body, attacking anything it came across.

In order to maintain its ever-growing body, he had to devour all in his path—whether human, Moujuu, or anything else. The count eradicated most of the Moujuu on the base's premises.

"I kinda wanna just leave him here and run," Giuli said apathetically.

Agreed, Yahiro thought.

Without any Japanese people to populate the area, the base's environs were nothing but desolate ruins. No civilians would die as a result of just leaving the count be.

And since there was a limit to his prey, eventually he wouldn't be able to sustain his constantly growing body, Lazarus or not. He would perish on his own soon enough. There was no need for Galerie Berith to risk their lives to destroy him.

Yet, Rosé rejected the idea with a sigh.

"The count would devour all traces of Sui Narusawa left on the base."

"Sui's traces...?"

"The data from the experiments conducted on her, I mean. Clues as to where she could've run to, as well. We would lose all that."

Are you okay with that? the blue-haired girl asked him with her eyes.

"So they turned him into this knowing all that?!" Yahiro grunted.

His sister's unending wickedness was dizzying. They had to kill this monster if they wanted to keep track of her. Avoid battle now and he would never catch up to her. There was only suffering awaiting no matter what choice he made. And she had built this conundrum herself by taking advantage of the count's greed.

"Don't worryyy! I will eeeat and defiiile eeevery single one of you equallyyy!"

More tentacles came out of the count's body. His growing form spilled into the base's building, grabbing and devouring Raimat employees hiding inside. They had to do something before he destroyed all traces of Sui, like Rosé said.

"What do we do?" Yahiro turned back to the twins while blocking a tentacle attack.

The count was already nearly fifteen meters in size and still expanding. It was only a matter of time before he swallowed the whole base. They had no time to carefully plan out a strategy.

"You kill him," Rosé replied, looking him straight in the eye.

Yahiro was taken aback by the too-simple plan.

"Me? What about Iroha?"

"Using the dragon's powers would only bring the dragon closer. Worst-case scenario, it could bring about a second genocide."

Yahiro kept quiet at Rosé's comment.

The dragon he'd seen four years back came to mind. A medium using the dragon's power was synonymous with summoning it. And there was no guarantee this dragon would obey Iroha. One could easily imagine it consuming her sense of self and unleashing its power unlimitedly.

"Still, if he's really a Lazarus, then he could regenerate from the tiniest piece of meat. I can't think of any way to kill that monster other than burning it up. I can't do it."

"There's no need to burn it entirely," Giuli said irresponsibly in response to Yahiro's calm analysis of the situation. "We just gotta destroy the core of his existence. Y'know, like, the count's soul."

"And where the hell is his soul?"

"How would I know? You're a Lazarus, too, though. Can't you tell?"

Yahiro clicked his tongue in reaction to her sloppy, abstract advice.

Still, something gnawed at him about it. If a Lazarus could recover from even a tiny bit of his body, then what would be the core as the base of his regeneration? His brain? His heart? Or would it really be something like Giuli suggested...his soul?

"Do you think Iroha's power could kill the count?" Rosé asked in a bizarrely calm tone.

"Y-yeah... I mean, why not?"

Iroha's flames had purified Sui's Ploutonions. There was no doubt that same power could burn the count to nothing. It was only natural for dragon powers to be able to kill a monster born out of dragon blood.

"Then you can also do it. The dragon medium can grant the Dragon Slayer her Regalia," she said without stuttering.

The girls offered up as sacrifice to the dragons bestowed the Dragon Slayers the power to do so. This was a motif repeated across many myths and legends. The Libyan queen tied the evil dragon up with her waistband; Kushinadahime transformed into a comb to join the battle against Susanoo.

These were all, obviously, myths. Fairy tales. However, the dragons and the Lazarus were real in this world–how different was that from a fairy tale?

"Why me? I'm sure there're people better fitted for the hero job."

"That won't do, unfortunately. The dragon can only offer the Regalia to the person–" Rosé cut herself off, then stood on her toes to get her lips closer to Yahiro's face. She whispered the rest into his ear.

"Huh...?" Yahiro opened his eyes wide.

Rosé rarely showed emotion on her face, which made the playful, naughty smile on her lips even more jarring.

Yahiro's eyes reflected indignation, embarrassment, and finally resignation as he glared at her.

It was then that he realized absolutely everything had been meticulously planned. He was being used, forced to cooperate with this wicked plot without his knowing, all along.

"I see... And you did it all for this from the very beginning."

"I think you should be thanking us, but in any case, we can hear your complaints later. But you must understand, Iroha bears no guilt."

"You... You're all going to hell," he cursed them, outraged.

Giuli stuck her tongue out like a kid playing a prank. Rosé, on the other hand, showed nothing but glee on her face.

"We'll be right there beside you."

"Go by yourselves!"

"Yahiro, what happened? Everything okay?! This isn't the time for arguing!" Iroha stood shakily, dismayed by their quarreling. Yahiro looked back at her with mixed feelings. "Wh-what?"

"Nothing. Stay away. I'll take care of that monster."

"Oh... O-okay. Good luck." Iroha nodded out of reflex, over-whelmed by Yahiro's fighting spirit.

He felt guilty about Iroha's trusting gaze, so he looked away.

Then he turned to face the count. Or rather, the thing that once was the count.

✝

Count Hector Raimat's thoughts were clearer than ever, in contrast to his slow and sluggish-looking body. Energy filled his aging body, blowing all fear of death into the distant past.

A sense of omnipotence took over the count, the craving for evolution dominating his mind.

There was this other kind of legend, just as, if not more, popular as the heroic tales of Dragon Slayers: stories where man becomes dragon.

After Sigurd slayed Fafnir, the hero transformed into a wyrm to protect the cursed gold originally.

The count knew he was drawing closer to these legends.

He was just barely keeping human form. He had grown huge, devouring many Moujuu and even whole armored vehicles, but his silhouette remained human. However, the dragon Ichor that brought about the transformation would make sure to complete its ultimate form—a dragon's. The abnormal multiplication of his cells was but the first step. He was like a caterpillar waiting to become a butterfly.

He did not find losing his human form lamentable in the least.

He had amassed more than enough power and riches across his long life as a merchant of death. He had already experienced all possible gratification for a human. Now, rather than seeking such pleasures, what he wished for the most was to defeat death—surpass humanity.

It was this desire that brought him this body—the dragon body beyond the limits of life.

He had no interest in the Regalia, which brought only destruction.

What he looked for was a dragon's vessel—the Ichor of a dragon summoned by a sacrificial medium.

It was then, after he obtained the Ichor and his transformation into wyrm began, that he remembered the Dragon Slayers. The individuals with the power to kill immortal dragons.

He wasn't ready yet. He was not a true Lazarus yet.

He needed the Regalia. A dragon treasure to protect.

A flash darted by the corner of his eye the moment he reached such a conclusion.

The monster shrieked at the sensation of burning pain—the fear of death he had forgotten.

†

"*Argh!* It's no use!" Yahiro yelled upon swinging his scarlet-hued katana.

The intense pain warned the count's Lazarus body of the risk of death: the aftereffect of the crimson flames engulfing his body.

A deep burn scar remained on the count's giant, hideously squirming body. The result of Yahiro's Blaze Regalia, as named by the Berith twins.

He managed to use it, but it was lacking in power. He had no idea where to aim to get to the count's soul.

The recoil was great, too. The power was but borrowed, and too much to handle even for the Lazarus. His entire body was screaming in pain after just one use. There was no way he could launch such attacks indefinitely.

"The Regalia! Theee! Regaliaaa! Give it to meee! That power is miiine!"

The count twisted his injured body, turning to Yahiro.

"–?!"

Yahiro fell to his knees, trying to dodge the barrage of tentacles.

Dammit, not now. Yahiro clicked his tongue. The death slumber— the backlash for using the Regalia. His whole body was devoid of strength. He couldn't dodge the attack.

"I won't let you!" Josh and his team fired, blowing the tentacles to bits.

Giuli's net bound the carrion, and Rosé's antimaterial rifle blew the count's face open with holes.

Everyone knew the counterattack would only momentarily slow the beast. That they delayed the count's swallowing of Yahiro by only a few seconds.

And these few seconds dropped Yahiro into a panic. Iroha, unarmed, ran up to him and held him tight.

"Yahiro!"

"Iroha?! What're you doing here?! Get away!" He tried mustering all his strength to shove her away.

Iroha looked right into his eyes and, with a strong smile on her face, said: "Remember that time!"

"…!" Memories came rushing back to him immediately.

He remembered the first time he'd used the Regalia, under that burning sunrise. He saw visions of Iroha holding a flaming sword, and he received it. She was clinging to him that time, too—their skin firmly touching each other.

"It'll be okay! I'm here by your side!"

Strength filled his body upon hearing her words.

The death slumber's fatigue cleared away, and instead, a blistering heat flowed from his body.

Then the count's giant body crashed down like an avalanche, swallowing both of them.

The deluge of carrion clung to them, hungering fiercely for their Regalia. But Yahiro was counting on that.

He knew not where the count's soul was, so the easiest move was to let him approach them. The count wanted to fuse with them, and so he had no choice but to come in direct contact. And by tracing back his open desire, they could reach his soul.

"Burn to ash… Blaze!"

Yahiro held the flaming sword tight and slashed the surrounding carrion, lust-polluted soul and all.

The wyrm, failure of a dragon that he was, exploded in a burst of purifying flames.

Putrid flesh the color of dried salmon flew every which way, decaying into miasma.

The hastily made scabbard mount of the katana broke away again.

The gunshots finally ceased, and silence spread throughout the base.

Yahiro held Iroha up before she collapsed from exhaustion and looked quietly at the sky.

Sui's helicopter was nowhere to be found. He had no idea in what direction it flew.

The sky was red, lit by the remaining flames. Sunset was close.

Iroha's hair fluttered in the wind.

The cicadas cried in the distance.

The summer clouds softly flew westward with the wind.

No dragon in the sky.

For now.

The cries of the cicadas echoed across the Japanese rock garden.

The chilly wind running through the vast bamboo grove came in through the open sliding screen, sounding the wind chime.

The wooden residence was reminiscent of an old Buddhist temple. At the center of the room sat Auguste Nathan. He was provided no cushion, and yet his back remained properly straight the whole time. He sat on the soles of his feet with perfect form.

Soon, the bamboo blind was rolled up, and a woman showed herself from the other side.

She wore a long *hakama*—luxurious Japanese trousers—in an outfit reminiscent of Heian-period clothing. Her long black hair reached her hips.

Her coat had a crest of a gold-winged bird—the Konjicho, symbol of the Imperial House.

She looked just barely above twenty. Her visage was graceful and gorgeous, but her expression was soft, like a mischievous kitten's.

"Did I make you wait, Auguste?" the woman casually called to the cordially sitting man. Her voice was gentle, like birdsong.

"No, you are just in time, Karura-sama," Nathan replied dryly, his head bowed.

Karura pouted discontentedly.

"Would you like a drink? I got my hands on some great gyokuro green tea."

"Thank you, but no."

"I have some snacks, too. I just got these from the Myojin main house."

"No, thank you."

Karura kept on trying to chat with him casually, but Nathan showed no intention of dropping the cordialities. She soon sighed with resignation and pursed her lips.

"Give me your report, Sir Nathan," Karura said solemnly, at sharp contrast with her previous tone.

Nathan nodded blankly and raised his head.

"Galerie Berith has secured Avaritia, the fire dragon hiding inside the 23 Wards. The Berith main house should be getting in contact with Ganzheit sooner or later."

"Galerie Berith…" Karura furrowed her brow in thought. "Not that surprising, I suppose."

"The Beriths are one of the oldest alchemist houses, after all. They are used to handling dragons." Nathan stated the information he was prepared to deliver without stuttering.

As dragons held a deep relationship with gold, alchemists were inevitably involved with them. The ouroboros, important symbol of the alchemists, was a dragon swallowing its own tail in the shape of a circle, and the god Mercury, considered the father of alchemy, was symbolized by a three-headed dragon.

"I understand. Those dolls will do well, but keep an eye on them," Karura responded, hiding her slight envy for the Berith twins.

Both sides were raised as birds in a cage, but they had the freedom to act as they pleased now; Karura admired them.

"They seemed to have taken care of our parting gift as well."

"Count Raimat... Poor soul. How many times did we warn him only destruction awaited beyond his desire for more power than he could handle?" Karura cast her eyes down out of pity for the late count.

Another agent had already reported to her of Hector Raimat's death after he took the Ichor. He turned into a wyrm, a false, incomplete dragon, and was burned to ash by Avaritia's Blaze Regalia.

A dragon was toxic, fanning the flames of greed in the human heart—it was only natural, in a sense, that the count's hunger for immortality would turn him into a wyrm. Sui Narusawa must have known that when handing him the Ichor; surely she was satisfied with the results.

"Did you get the F-med data?"

"Yes. I've made the salvaged data public in the foundation's archives. I thought setting the confidentiality level too high would in turn produce needless speculation."

"That's fine. Better for the greedy army men to know the Fafnir soldiers are no alternative for the Lazarus." Karura smiled in satisfaction.

Nathan wasn't looking to make practical use of the Fafnir soldiers. His goal, his mission, was the opposite: to prove that they were useless as weapons—that they fell far short of the Lazarus.

His mission had been accomplished thanks to Yahiro Narusawa. Now no armies would try to use dragon blood as a weapon for a good long while. After all, a single Lazarus boy had easily destroyed an entire company of Fafnir soldiers.

"With Avaritia's arrival, we now have six pieces on the board. Only the heaven and lightning are missing... The quick-tempered lot are sure to make their move soon." Karura's eyes glinted coldly.

Four years after the J-nocide, she had finally figured out the identities of six dragon mediums. But this country need not six whole dragons. They had to be slayed. By a hero.

"There is something more I want to report," Nathan said after a slight indecisive silence.

"I'll allow it. Go on," Karura ordered with familiarity.

Nathan nodded, then took a breath.

"Superbia...appears to be weakening after all. Her inconsistent sleep cycles continue even now, and they have been growing in frequency. I believe she won't be able to unleash as much power as she did four years ago anymore."

"Do we know why?"

"This is merely speculation on my part, but it might be related to Yahiro Narusawa continuing to be a Lazarus."

Flames burned behind his emotionless eyes, but only for just a moment. He was back to being inexpressive after the following blink.

"I see. That is quite the interesting report indeed."

Karura mouthed the boy's name and smiled brightly.

✝

"Oh, Dear Brother... I so love you," the girl whispered in the cold rain.

Her middle school uniform was drenched.

Fresh blood was pouring incessantly from her left wrist.

Standing on the rooftop of the building still under construction, she turned around with a faint smile.

Clear tears overflowed from her eyes, reflecting only despair.

The boy called her name. He pleaded with a serious expression, yet his voice did not reach her.

The wind blew, her white hair fluttering softly in the air.

Then she said her last words.

Her voice calm, like in prayer. Her lips twisted in a mad smile.

"This whole world should perish for not allowing us to be together."

†

Yahiro found his hideout drab after returning for the first time in a couple of days.

The ruins of the private university campus were by the outskirts of the 23 Wards. He thought he had gotten entirely used to sleeping in the lab, but now it felt so alien.

He realized he felt like this because the noisy twins and the rest of Galerie Berith and, most of all, Iroha, weren't there, but he tried to avoid thinking about it.

He didn't mind being tricked or betrayed, but he couldn't stand to lose the precious things he'd gathered. If he'd lose them in the end anyway, then he was better off not having them in the first place. A trite thought, for sure, but he really felt that way.

Yahiro had lived all alone for four long years. He did not want to admit the people he'd spent time with for just one or two days could affect him this much.

But perhaps once he had thought of it, it was already too late. And he was aware of this.

"What am I supposed to do? It was them who reached out." Yahiro muttered excuses.

He didn't want any burden. He didn't want what he held dear stolen from him. He didn't want to let them go himself.

But considering his Lazarus body, he would inevitably lose them all one day. Then why not reach back out to them for that short while, even if on a whim?

Besides, they were useful. He needed Iroha and Galerie Berith in order to accomplish his mission: finding and killing Sui Narusawa.

His sister kept on taking too many lives. Killing her was his only and last wish. He wanted nothing but to stop the mad girl who said she loved him.

His hands couldn't handle carrying anything more.

He only reached back out to them in order to use them. Or that was the plan.

"..."

Yahiro shook his head, feeling stupid for even thinking about this whole thing.

He didn't come back to his hideout to bask in silly sentimentality. He was there to vacate the place. To collect his things in order to travel with Galerie Berith.

"Not that I have much to take with me."

The few amounts of foreign currency he had saved up across four years and a change of clothes was everything he had. That and his old modded phone.

He reached his finger to boot up the solar-powered smartphone out of habit and chuckled at himself for doing so.

He would never again watch the Iroha Waon live streams he loved so much. He couldn't enjoy those videos sincerely now that he knew her real identity. Not now that he knew what Iroha was like in real life.

Not that he disliked her. Quite the opposite, he found her far more attractive than he had ever imagined.

Okay, I guess I can watch one last video...

Yahiro convinced himself, saying he would only put it on as background noise, but as soon as he booted the phone up...

"Waooon!"

"Uwoh?!" Yahiro shrieked upon hearing Iroha's voice in his ear.

He turned around and found her holding her hands up to her head like animal ears and a smirk on her face.

"Ah-ha-ha-ha! Did that scare you? It totally did! Hi, everywaon!"

"...Iroha... What're you doing in here?! We're in the middle of the 23 Wards!" Yahiro yelled completely seriously at her for showing up in the danger zone crawling with Moujuu.

Iroha, though, burst into laughter as if it was a joke.

"Did you forget the 23 Wards are my turf? Nuemaru's here, so there's no danger."

"I doubt he'd be of much use..." Yahiro sighed as he saw the dog-size Raiju at her feet.

The white beast reacted to his words and glared at him, sparks flying all around him.

"Hmm...so this is where you lived. It does smell like you." Iroha dived onto the sofa without question and buried her face in the sheets.

"Stop sniffing my bed, you animal!"

"Hey, is this your phone? Mind if I see your gallery?"

"I do mind. Why do you wanna see my photos in the first place?"

"I'm just wondering if you took screenshots of my videos." She raised her head, grinning.

Yahiro smiled awkwardly. "Why would I do that?"

"Well, there are many reasons, but I've heard boys like looking at pictures of the girl they like for lewd purposes."

"Who said I like you?" He scowled at her for her baseless fabrications. He felt offended at the accusation that he watched the streams because of such romantic feelings. "First of all, I just can't see Waon sexually, y'know? She wasn't that for me."

"R-really...? Oh, so you're more serious about this, I see; I shouldn't be joking, then..."

"Wha—? Serious?"

"O-oh my... You make me blush, hearing that directly to my face... Ah-ha-ha..." Iroha's face turned red up to her ears. Seemed she couldn't handle direct expressions of love despite her exaggeratedly high self-esteem.

"You're getting it wrong. I mean that I saw her as, like, a pet or family."

"Family..."

"She's also super dumb, so."

"Wha—?! Why?! What's dumb about me?!" Iroha froze up in shock.

Yahiro's modded phone finished booting. It showed his lock screen, the background picture changing randomly every so often, and it just happened to change then into an ordinary family photo at the beach.

A boy, his parents, and his little sister, the latter looking nervous. Iroha's face stiffened upon realizing it was Yahiro's family.

"...Sorry... I didn't mean to see. I'm so sorry..."

"No, it's fine. I forgot I set it." Yahiro shook his head, not minding it at all.

It wasn't a picture he couldn't show other people. Even though his parents were no longer in this world.

"This is a picture from the day we took Sui in...," Yahiro said, staring at the girl in the picture.

Iroha gasped. She bit her lip and cast her eyes down for a while before finally mustering her courage and raising her head.

"Yahiro, do you wish to go back to the world before the J-nocide?"

"Huh?"

Iroha kept her eyes set on Yahiro's as she grabbed his hands.

"...I have no family. I have no memories of when I was little. I was in the institute as far back as I can remember... So actually, I'm glad I got so many brothers and sisters after the J-nocide."

Yahiro forgot how to breathe for a second upon hearing her confession.

A solitary girl without memories of her past. She was just like Sui.

Sui didn't know her real parents or her birthplace. They couldn't find any trace of how she had survived up until that point. It was as though she had wandered into this world all of a sudden from somewhere else far away.

Was that really a coincidence? Both dragon mediums sharing such circumstances?

Iroha noticed the confusion in Yahiro's face.

"But they all had real families. They could've lived more happily. You think if I fought the other dragon girls and became the last one standing, then I really would be able to create a world as I wish...? What should I do?" Her voice became frailer and more intermittent as she went on.

Iroha petted Nuemaru, sitting on her knees, as she hung her head in silence.

Yahiro stared at her shapely face and sighed.

He remembered what Rosé had said in the middle of the battle against the count.

Yahiro had asked her why he was able to use the Regalia, and the blue-haired girl responded:

"The dragon can only offer the Regalia to the person its medium has fallen in love with."

"Do as you please."

The answer came out of Yahiro's mouth before he could even think about it.

Iroha's eyes widened in surprise.

Yahiro faced the other way, avoiding her eyes.

"I said this before. Just do whatever you want. And if any other dragons get in your way, I'll be by your side, protecting you."

"Thanks..." Iroha nodded awkwardly.

Her eyes stayed wide as tears began to well. Yahiro braced himself for another session of loud crying. He was used to getting yelled at, hated on, and even killed, but he just couldn't get used to seeing Iroha cry, and he likely never would. Seeing her like that hurt his chest more than even the sharpest blade.

He prayed hard for her to stop, and the heavens listened. She shed no tears in the end—because someone else entered the room before she could.

"Did you hear that, Rosy? He's so cool!"

"Admirable indeed. I take it as a formal contract in which he guarantees Iroha Mamana's safety in the event of a dragon attack. Let us add that clause to his contract with the Galerie."

"...What're you guys doing in here?" Yahiro huffed at the sight of the twins appearing out of nowhere and spouting nonsense to his face.

"We're here to guard Iroha, as well as help you move out. You think she'd come here alone?" Rosé sighed.

Shrewd Giuli noticed the laptop on the desk. "Wow! A PC! Hey, can I check your pictures folder?"

"Stop it! No way!" Yahiro was clearly shaken this time, unlike when asked the same question for his phone.

He rushed over to the PC, but Giuli was faster.

Iroha burst into laughter at the sight of his restlessness. She heartily laughed as though all previous concerns had been blown away. She held her sides and wiped her tears before reaching her left hand out to Yahiro. A smile still in her eyes, she asked, with the most serious tone she could muster:

"Yahiro, pinkie promise me."

"Okay? Pinkie promise you what, though?" he asked, surrendering the other matter.

He couldn't say no after Iroha had seen him do the same thing with Giuli. He doubted she would get jealous of the other girl, but it wasn't hard to imagine her clashing with the twin as a result later on, and most of all, he didn't want her crying because of it.

He knew his cursed Lazarus hands, dirtied with blood, shouldn't be carrying more than necessary. But were he to reject the hand reaching out for him, then he would forget he was once human—he would become a real monster through and through.

The inner conflict was clear on his face, and so Iroha gazed at him like she would a child in need of protection.

"Stay by my side until I make my wish come true."

"That's too vague, don't you think?" Yahiro frowned in request for something more precise.

The current terms were unclear enough that this pact could very well go on for eternity.

Iroha realized this and nodded in agreement.

"Okay, then let's put it this way." Iroha wrapped her pinkie finger around Yahiro's.

Then she drew her head closer, until only their breaths filled the space between them.

Yahiro felt the dragon medium's powers flowing into him from their intertwined fingers.

The power to destroy the world. A cursed power that drove so many people to death.

Yet even so, he knew the promise would be fulfilled.

He knew her oh-so-simple wish of staying by his side would be granted.

For the Lazarus would make sure of it.

For he would protect her until the promised time arrived.

Iroha narrowed her eyes mischievously and said those innocent, beautiful words—the spell that bound them.

"Until death do us part."

Afterword

This book's original title, *Utsuro naru Regalia*, at first was supposed to be written out in *hiragana*, since I considered the *kanji* for *Utsuro* too hard to read, not to mention the abbreviation, but in the end, everyone told me that writing it in *hiragana* was too uncool and boring, so we went for the *kanji* title. And sure enough, seeing the abbreviation *UtsuRega* written out in *hiragana* started looking off to me, but then someone saw an ad with the *kanji* writing and they asked me, "What's *Kyoro naru* mean?" and I just wanted to pluck my hairs out. *Kyoro naru...* Damn *Kyoro naru...*

Anyway, I hope you enjoyed *Hollow Regalia*, Volume 1.

This is my first new series in a while, after *Strike the Blood*. I am sorry if you have been waiting a long time for something new from me, but finally, here it is.

I had a hard time getting used to this new world and characters. I wrote a ton of reference documents, and I had to rewrite the manuscript more times than I'd ever done before. But thanks to all that hard work, I ended up loving Yahiro, Iroha, and all the other characters. At first, I was planning to have a more stylish protagonist, but he ended up dumber, er, I mean, more impudent than I thought. But, well, I suppose you can't survive in such a dreary world without a certain level of boldness.

So the main theme of this series is dragon vs. dragon slayer. Fantasy, pretty much. Truth be told, my debut work with Dengeki Bunko was also about dragons and dragon slayers... Don't call it lack of growth. I call it going back to my roots.

To be completely honest, dragons have always been one of my favorite motifs in the fantasy genre. Be it in books, movies, or anime, seeing cool, strong dragons always gets me hyped up. I love Western and Eastern dragons equally. Lately I've seen many dragons used as fodder in recent games, and that makes me sad, but I suppose that's another way to enjoy them. You can fight them, you can ride them, or you can even eat them. Dragons are great in all forms. But, well, when I put them into my works, I want them to be overwhelming and majestic; that's how *Hollow Regalia* came to be.

Oh, I should also mention: The Japanese die out all of a sudden at the beginning of this story, but that doesn't mean I hate them, no. Just take it as another version of a postapocalyptic setting. I just find the idea of exploring the land, map in hand, while fighting monsters on the way, to be quite fun.

I want to thank Miyuu for the illustrations—the wonderful designs far exceeded my imagination. I shivered and sobbed when I first saw the drawings. I am looking forward to continuing to work together.

I also want to thank everyone who was involved in the creation of this book. My deepest gratitude.

And of course, thank you for reading it!

I am already writing the second volume. I'm hoping to get it to you as fast as I can. Until we meet again!

Gakuto Mikumo

02
**Dragons and
the Deep Blue Sea**

HOLLOW
REGALIA

Yahiro Narusawa—Lazarus

Kuyo Masakane

DATA

Age:	17	**Birthday**	8/16
Height:	5'7"		
Traits:	Black hair and eyes, 134 lbs.		
Special Skill:	Kendo (first kyu)		
Likes:	Yakitori, watching movies		
Dislikes:	Onions, classical literature		

SUMMARY

He became a Lazarus after being bathed in dragon blood. One of the few surviving Japanese. He lived on his own as a salvager, retrieving antiques and artwork from the quarantined 23 Wards. He continues to look for his younger sister, Sui Narusawa, who went missing after the J-nocide.

Iroha Mamana—Moujuu Tamer

DATA

Age:	17	**Birthday**	7/21 (tentative)
Height:	5'3"		
Traits:	Brown hair and eyes, F-cup or greater		
Special Skill:	Streaming, cosplay		
Likes:	*Dorayaki*, family		
Dislikes:	Coffee, math		

SUMMARY

A Japanese girl who survived near the center of the quarantined 23 Wards. She lives with her seven brothers and sisters in the former site of the Tokyo Dome. Sentimental and quick to cry. She has the power to control Moujuu and is targeted by private military companies because of it.

Iroha Waon—Streamer

Age:	17,000	**Birthday**	7/21	**Height:**	15 apples
Traits:	Silver hair, green eyes, furry ears and tail				

Cosplayer who live streams in Japanese on a foreign streaming site. Despite her cute looks and voice, the actual contents of her videos are not very interesting; she's having trouble increasing her followers. There seems to be a special reason why she continues to stream despite the low viewership...

Giulietta Berith
Simpleminded Martial Artist

Age:	16	**Birthday**	6/13
Height:	5′1″		
Traits:	Orange highlights, E-cup		
Special Skill:	All martial arts		
Likes:	Fruit, art appreciation		
Dislikes:	Blobby things, grotesque things		

Executive of arms dealer Galerie Berith. Older twin sister of Rosetta. She's of Chinese descent but a citizen of Belgium, base of the House of Berith. She overpowers Yahiro in hand-to-hand combat with superhuman skill. She is friendly and respected by her underlings.

Rosetta Berith
Coolheaded Sniper

Age:	16	**Birthday**	6/13
Height:	5′1″		
Traits:	Blue highlights, less than A-cup		
Special Skill:	Sniping		
Likes:	Black tea, reading		
Dislikes:	Alcohol, horror movies		

Executive of arms dealer Galerie Berith. Younger twin sister of Giulietta. She has superhuman physical ability and a natural talent for weaponry, especially firearms. The opposite of her sister, she is always calm and collected and rarely shows any emotions. She usually takes command of the troops. She always dotes on her sister, Giulietta.

CONFIDENTIAL

Josh Keegan
Upbeat Former Cop

Age:	25	Birthday	7/2
Height:	5′6″	Traits:	Blond hair and blue eyes

Galerie Berith operator. American of Irish descent. Former cop targeted by a criminal organization. Jokey personality but an excellent soldier.

Paola Resente
Pretty Soldier

Age:	24	Birthday	5/16
Height:	5′7″	Traits:	Brunette and hazel eyes

Galerie Berith operator. Mexican. Former actress with a loyal fan base. She works hard to send money back to her family in her homeland.

Yang Wei
Quiet Avenger

Age:	27	Birthday	9/24
Height:	6′0″	Traits:	Black hair and black eyes

Operator of Galerie Berith. Chinese. His father, a high-ranking government official, was murdered, and while investigating the case, he came across Ganzheit and subsequently joined Galerie Berith. He is handsome, and usually a gentle man but becomes scary when mad.

Sui Narusawa
Earth Dragon Medium

Age:	16	Birthday	12/14 (tentative)

Height:	4′11″

Traits:	White hair and red eyes, 82 lbs.

Younger sister of Yahiro Narusawa. She is a medium with the power to summon dragons and responsible for the J-nocide. She fell into a deep slumber after getting injured during the aforementioned event. Currently under Ganzheit's custody, acting as their guinea pig in exchange for protection.

Auguste Nathan
Ganzheit Agent

Age:	29	Birthday	2/9

Height:	6′2″	Traits:	Black hair and amber eyes

Japanese doctor of African descent and agent of Ganzheit. He uses the dragon medium for his experiments, giving her protection and granting her wishes in exchange.

Hector Raimat

Arms Dealer

Age:	74	**Birthday**	10/3
Height:	6′7″	**Traits:**	Gray hair and brown eyes

Chairman of the leading weapons manufacturer: Raimat International. Bona fide noble with the title of count. Provides a lab for Nathan and goes after Iroha in order to obtain the power of immortality granted by dragon blood.

Firman La Hire

Arrogant Fafnir Soldier

Age:	28	**Birthday**	3/16
Height:	5′6″	**Traits:**	Blond hair and green eyes

Commander in chief of the Japanese branch of RMS, a private military company affiliated with Raimat International. He graduated from a military academy as the top student and became the youngest major in the army. He is an ambitious elite commander who volunteers to be a test subject for the F-med.

KEY WORDS

Galerie Berith

European trading company. They mostly deal in weapons and military technology. This deadly dealer has its own private military for protection. Funded by the Marquis House of Berith.

Ganzheit

Supranational organization that aims to protect humanity from disaster brought about by dragons. They have passed on records and memories of past dragon appearances and own many divine instruments.

Fafnir Soldiers

Soldiers of the RMS private military company enhanced with a special drug called the F-med. They undergo draconization, which grants them dramatically superior strength, agility, and regenerative ability. As a downside, draconization also makes them more violent and reduces the life span of their cells.

Area of Operations Map

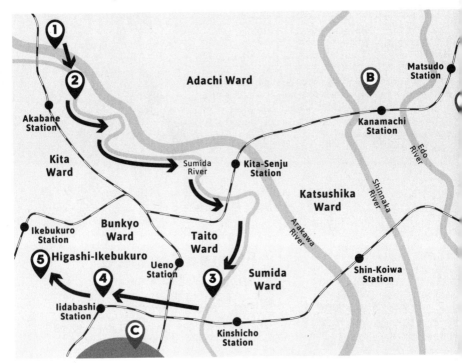

Key Points List

A:	Ed's store	near Matsudo Station
B:	Yahiro's base	the former site of Rikkyo University
C:	The Ploutonion	one-mile radius from the National Diet Building

Route for Operation: Kushinada Hunt

1:	Starting point of operations	Arakawa Riverside
2:	Galerie Berith Route	Sumida River
3:	Battle against the Moujuu "Bā Xià"	Sumida River by Kuramae Bridge
4:	Destination of Operation: Kushinada Hunt	former site of the Tokyo Dome
5:	Battle against the Fafnir soldiers	Higashi-Ikebukuro

Glossary

Immortals/Lazarus

Humans who have obtained the power of immortality by bathing in dragon blood. Does not include eternal youth. The power will not activate under a certain damage threshold (bloodshed required, generally). Not everyone who comes in contact with dragon blood will become immortal—one must meet certain conditions.

Lazarus bodies react to lethal danger by materializing an armor called the Goreclad. Each Goreclad manifests a different extra effect according to their Regalia.

Dragons

Supernatural beings of myth and legend throughout the world. They bring about great disaster while also granting blessings. A dragon is the world itself—legend says the world we live in was born from a dragon's corpse. Mediums frequently appear in dragon stories as sacrifices. The dragons descend to earth through the body of these women; some understand it as the mediums summoning them from another realm.

Regalia

General term for the powers of a dragon. These special powers overturn the laws of physics and bring disaster to the world. Only when a Lazarus is near a dragon medium or divine instrument, a relic of the dragon, may they use the Regalia of their root dragon.

The J-nocide

Refers to both the meteorite fall that caused natural disasters throughout Japan, as well as the massacre of the Japanese people that ensued throughout the world. Save for a very few exceptions, Japanese people died out.

Moujuu

Mysterious monsters that appeared throughout Japan at the time of the J-nocide. They are beyond our understandings of living organisms and cannot be easily suppressed with modern weaponry. It is said that the majority of people within Japan died by their hands. The blood of the Lazarus is lethally toxic to Moujuu.

The Ploutonion

A giant pit that appeared at the heart of Tokyo's 23 Wards following the J-nocide. It is said its dark depths connect to the underworld. As swarms of Moujuu come out of the Ploutonion, the 23 Wards have been sealed and quarantine.

Celebratory Illustration

I HAD FUN DRAWING FOR THIS. I LOVE IROHA AND YAHIRO'S RELATIONSHIP, SO I CAN'T WAIT TO SEE WHERE IT GOES!

MIYUU

Congratulations on the release of *Hollow Regalia*!
I was very excited to see Mikumo's new series!
I will be following it as a fan. Iroha's knee socks
are so delightful. I'm glad I got to draw her!

HAVE YOU BEEN TURNED ON TO LIGHT NOVELS YET?